By CONNIE BAILEY

NOVELS
Kaji Sukoshi and the Shining One
Miles to Go
Moonlight, Tiger, and Smoke
Revenant
Serendipity Kit
Something for Nothing
True Blue
Until It's Time to Go

NOVELLAS
Human After All
Insert Here
The Raw Prawn

Published by DREAMSPINNER PRESS
http://www.dreamspinnerpress.com

SERENDIPITY
KIT

CONNIE BAILEY

Dreamspinner Press

Published by
Dreamspinner Press
5032 Capital Circle SW
Suite 2, PMB# 279
Tallahassee, FL 32305-7886
USA
http://www.dreamspinnerpress.com/

Serendipity Kit
© 2013 Connie Bailey.

Cover Art
© 2013 Paul Richmond.
http://www.paulrichmondstudio.com
Cover content is for illustrative purposes only and any person depicted on the cover is a model.

ISBN: 978-1-62798-268-9
Digital ISBN: 978-1-62798-267-2

Printed in the United States of America
First Edition
December 2013

ACKNOWLEDGMENTS

My thanks to the staff of Dreamspinner Press for their talent, hard work, and for always listening to my opinion with respect.

CHAPTER

ONE

"HELLO? IS anyone here?"

Romy slid out from under the car he was working on and got to his feet. Grabbing a rag off the workbench, he wiped his hands as he walked to the front of the two-bay garage. In the open doorway was a hazy-edged silhouette.

"Can I help you?" Romy asked.

The visitor came into the building and Romy's eyes widened at the choice of clothing… especially in this part of Houston. The slender man looked to be around the same age as Romy—past twenty-one but still well shy of thirty—but that's the only thing they appeared to have in common.

Romy was wearing dark-blue coveralls over a white tank top and boxers and his long black hair was pulled back in a careless ponytail. The stranger was dressed in snug jeans decorated with metal studs all the way down the sides to where they tucked into a pair of pale-blue cowboy boots. His long-sleeved pullover was pink, fuzzy, and so loosely woven that Romy could see the strappy T-shirt underneath it. His auburn hair was a perfectly tousled short pageboy and diamonds sparkled in both earlobes. Romy couldn't believe this guy had made it from his car to the garage without getting beaten up.

"How can I help you?" Romy restated his question.

"There's something wrong with my car."

Romy focused on his potential customer's face and it was a moment before he answered. He'd never seen a man this beautiful, except in glossy-magazine cologne ads. The guy had bone structure like geometry, big doe eyes, and lips that courted kisses.

"What seems to be the trouble?" Romy asked.

"It just stopped."

"Just stopped?"

"Yeah. It didn't make any weird noises or anything. I had my foot on the gas, but it just kept getting slower until it stopped."

"Sounds like you have a clogged filter. Where is it?"

"I don't have any idea."

Romy's brows drew together in a frown. "You forgot where you left your car?"

"No. I know where the car is, but I don't know where the filter is."

Romy decided to start over. "I'm Jerome O'Keefe, but everybody calls me Romy," he said, offering his hand. "Welcome to O'Keefe's Garage."

"Christopher Britten, everyone calls me Kit." Kit shook Romy's hand briefly and played along with the charade. "I'm having trouble with my car. Can you help me?"

"If I can, I certainly will." Romy smiled. "You're not from around here, are you?"

"My sister asked me to drive down and pick up something for her. I'm not exactly lost, but...."

"If you don't mind me saying so, after I fix your car, you might want to turn around and go back the way you came."

"Why?"

Romy gave Kit his patented *are you high?* look. "It's kind of a rough part of town, and the way you're dressed—"

"Is there something wrong with my clothes?"

"I didn't say that, but there are guys around here that would kick your ass for that shirt."

"If someone wants my shirt that bad, I'll give it to them. I can always get another one. My sister sells them in her store."

"I meant you might get your ass kicked for *wearing* that shirt."

"Oh." Kit paused before he spoke again. "You're not one of those guys, are you?" he asked, only half-joking. After all, he was in an unfamiliar part of town and it did look a little dodgy.

"Nope. So where's your car?"

Kit smiled in relief. So, this attractive mechanic wasn't really scowling at him—it was just a trick of the man's dark eyebrows that drew down over his even darker eyes. Honestly, this face belonged on a fiery, sword-wielding bandit fighting injustice and Spanish land barons.

"The car?" Romy prompted.

Kit snapped out of fantasy mode, something he found himself doing several times a day. "It's outside."

"Well, obviously, but how far away is it?"

"Right outside. I pushed it here when I saw your body-shop sign down the street."

Pushed it here? Romy took another look at the pretty-boy and noted that the body under the girly clothes looked very fit. "This isn't a body shop," he said, when Kit gave him a curious look. "It's a garage. I don't pound fenders. I fix engines. Now, let's go have a look at yours."

Kit stood there for a second, watching Romy walk away, before he hurried to catch up.

Romy whistled when he caught sight of Kit's car. "Are you rich or something?" he asked as they crossed the small parking lot with gravel crunching underfoot.

"Me? Not really."

"Then how do you afford this?" Romy ran a hand lovingly down the front fender of the red Ferrari California.

"Birthday present from my mom and dad." Kit smiled. *"They're rich."*

"Man, I'd love a car like this." Romy bent down to peer in the window and straightened up again. "But not in red."

"Why not red?" Kit asked automatically as he watched Romy. The way the mechanic stroked the car was downright sexy, arousing even.

"Because it screams *pull me over* to the cops, and this car already looks like it's doing sixty while it's sitting still."

Kit smiled, glad the mechanic was making an attempt to be personable. He was not a fan of the brusque exchanges his father referred to as *professional behavior.* "What color would you like?" he asked to keep the conversation going. His easy manner aside, Romy O'Keefe was still a very attractive package, and Kit was already trying to think of a way to find out if he was gay.

"The California comes in a really nice blue, but I think I'd like black," Romy said as he reached in the car for the hood release. "Want to know when my birthday is?"

Kit chuckled, and a pleasant shiver zinged through Romy's body as though a cool breeze had caressed his bare skin. Romy swallowed as he recognized the symptoms—nerves, shyness, curiosity—of a sudden onset of severe lust. Oh well, there wasn't much he could do about it, except try to keep cool.

"Let's have a look at her." Romy opened the hood, cringing at the lame words coming out of his mouth.

Kit leaned in to look at the engine, too, his head just a few centimeters from Romy's. He didn't say anything to distract Romy as he examined the engine; he just wanted to watch. There was something indefinably, undeniably sensuous in the way Romy occasionally reached out to physically inspect a part, his long fingers moving with competence and grace. When Romy looked up, Kit felt a small shock as their eyes met. He sincerely hoped this man was gay, because everything about Romy made Kit want to fuck him.

"Get in," Romy said.

Kit blinked. "What?"

"Try to start the car."

"Right." Kit got into the front seat, leaving the door open. "Be cool, Kit," he said under his breath. "Don't start drooling and babbling like a schoolgirl with a crush." He pumped the gas pedal three times, as he always did before pushing the ignition button. "Just because Romy O'Keefe is the sexiest guy you've ever met is no reason to lose your mind." He turned the key and the starter engaged, but the engine refused to turn over.

"Okay," Romy called. "You can stop now."

Kit climbed out of the car. "Do you know what's wrong with it?"

"I'm pretty sure I do." Romy didn't speak again until he'd removed the fuel filter. "Give me a minute," he said, as he carried the filter into the garage.

Kit hovered in the doorway until Romy returned. "Can you fix it?" he asked.

"It had about a gazillion ant corpses in it. I don't have any idea how they got into your tank, but they're gone now."

"That's kind of freaky."

"It happens more often than you'd think."

"Now it's kind of creepy."

"Yeah. Makes you wonder what the little boogers were up to." Romy smiled. "I can install a new filter and get you back on the road real quick. It's not made for a Ferrari, but it'll work until you can get the car to your regular mechanic."

"You have time to do that now?"

"It's not a big job."

Kit stood to the side as Romy replaced the part. Shamelessly, he indulged a few fantasies while he watched the muscles of Romy's broad shoulders, long back, and compact ass moving under the stretched-tight material of the coveralls. Kit was a little disappointed when Romy straightened up and turned toward him.

"There you go," Romy said.

"All finished?" Kit asked, hoping Romy didn't notice the bulge in Kit's jeans.

"All done," Romy confirmed.

"Thanks. What do I owe you?"

"Not a thing. It only took two minutes."

"That's ridiculous. If you don't want money for your labor, you have to at least let me pay you for the part."

"Honestly, it was nothing. I have a whole crate of them."

"But you're running a business here! You can't just give things away."

"My mom taught me to do at least one kind thing a day, but I can see you feel strongly about this," Romy drawled. "Want to draw up a business plan for me and set up a stock portfolio?"

"Are you making fun of me?" Kit asked. In fact, he suspected that Romy was flirting with him, but he wasn't quite sure yet. And in Texas, you wanted to be 100 percent sure about things like that.

"Nope, not at all."

"Then tell me what I owe you."

Romy suppressed a smile at the cute look of frustration on Kit's face. "I will."

"You *will*?"

"You can do me a favor someday, okay?"

"Who do you think you are? The Godfather?"

Romy's laugh was made of very white teeth against very red lips. "You just recognized me?"

"All right," Kit said, after a few moments' thought. "I owe you one."

"See if the car starts first."

Kit got into the Ferrari and turned it on. The engine started up and ran smoothly.

"That's a beautiful sound," Romy said admiringly. "You're good to go."

"I wonder if I could use your bathroom."

"Sure, it's in the office."

Kit was happy to find Romy still admiring the Ferrari when he came back from the bathroom. Reaching in the car, he found his bag and took out a small case. "Here's my number," he said, handing a business card to Romy.

Romy tucked the card into his breast pocket. "A real beauty," he said, pretending he was talking about the car.

Kit hesitated, waiting for Romy to say something else, but the mechanic didn't add anything to his observation. "Well... 'bye for now," Kit said, breaking the silence.

Romy nodded, and Kit shut the door. Maneuvering the sports car through a three-point turn, Kit watched Romy in the rearview mirror. Reluctantly, Kit shifted up and left the parking lot for the street. His gaze went to the side mirror, but Romy was already walking back into the garage. *Forget about him,* Kit chided himself. *You're just horny and he's smokin' hot. Things like instant rapport and love at first sight only happen in songs, and books, and movies. They don't exist in real life.*

But he fixed your car for nothing, Kit's ever-hopeful libido chimed in. *Why would he do that if he didn't want to boink you?*

"Maybe he's just a nice guy," Kit said. Abruptly realizing he was talking to himself again, he turned on the radio.

Romy patted his breast pocket and felt the resistance of the rectangle of crisp paper. He had the angel's phone number. Maybe miracles did happen after all. It had been quite a while since anyone had made Romy's heart beat fast, and even if nothing came of it, the encounter had livened up his day.

When Kit and Romy went to their separate beds that night, each lay awake wondering if the other was interested in him.

CHAPTER

TWO

IT WAS the time between the morning rush of customers and the two-to-four stream of casual shoppers. Lunch had been eaten, and Alla Moda, the upscale boutique owned by Kit's sister Eliza, was quiet. The only sounds were those of small talk as small tasks were performed to freshen the decor. Kit sighed audibly and his sister looked up from her work.

"Are you going to tell me?" Eliza asked.

"Tell you what?"

"The reason you're so distracted." She reached over and took his hand, halting his fidgeting. "And the reason you're shredding that flower arrangement."

Kit met her eyes. "Sorry," he said. "Have I been a monumental pain in the ass?"

"Excuse me?" Eliza paused, the white rose in her hand hovering over the fleur-de-lis-shaped vase. She was fifteen years older than Kit and often treated him more like a son than a brother. And she tolerated no vulgar language in her store, even the mildest.

"Sorry," Kit said again. "Have I been completely useless today?"

"Never. Even when you aren't working, you're quite decorative."

Kit smiled. "It always makes me feel better when you compliment my looks. Does that make me shallow?"

"You're beautiful, little brother. Don't obsess over it, just enjoy it."

"Do you really think I'm obsessing?"

"It's one of your defining character traits. So, what are you fascinated with at the moment?"

"Remember when you sent me to get the brocade for those drapes?"

Eliza glanced at the elegant new window treatment at the front of her shop. "Of course I remember. It was only a few days ago. I worked all night hanging those drapes."

"My car broke down and—"

"You didn't tell me that!"

Kit's gaze went to the flowers Eliza was arranging. "It's no big deal. I just wanted to keep it to myself for a while."

"Why?"

"The guy that fixed it—"

Eliza interrupted again. "How did I know there would be a guy in this story?"

"I only talked to him for about fifteen minutes while he fixed the car, but I can't get him out of my head." Kit looked up at his sister. "Do you need any more fabric?"

"You don't need an excuse to drive by his place. You're a grown man. Just go see him, if that's what you want."

"In case it slipped your mind, gay stalkers are somewhat frowned upon in the great state of Texas. I need a plausible reason to visit the garage."

"Well, you have about a dozen cars, don't you?"

"You're exaggerating."

"It's what I do."

Kit looked around the tastefully lavish boutique. "Splendidly," he said.

"So... why do you need a made-up reason to see this man? Besides a justified fear of getting bashed?"

Kit hesitated before he spoke. "I don't know if he's gay."

"Oh, Kissy, please don't fall for another straight man. I couldn't stand seeing your heart broken like that again."

"I'll be careful," Kit promised and hurried on. "But you should see him. He's perfect."

"Then be brave and talk to him. Somewhere public. Or hire a private detective."

"I've certainly given it a lot of thought."

"That explains the constant bulge."

Kit stared at Eliza. "Excuse me?"

"Sorry. That *was* vulgar of me." Eliza hid her smile behind the bouquet as she turned to set the vase on a marble column. "But if you want peace of mind, talk to him."

"I'm sort of waiting for *him* to call *me*. I gave him my card."

"Kissy, you know I'd never interfere in your personal life, even if I do think you'd be happier if you stopped all this boy-chasing nonsense. But that's your business. All I can do is give you my best advice. It's up to you whether you follow it." Eliza removed a drooping rose from the vase. "Go after what you want, but don't sit around whining about it. That gets you nothing."

Kit sighed. "Do you have any more work for me today?"

"Did you bring the cashmere shawls out of the back?"

"The box is behind the counter."

"The plants are watered?"

Kit nodded.

"I can't think of anything else, unless you want to finish here."

Kit glanced at the sheaves of roses, gladioli, and ferns, and the line of vases waiting to contain them. "I'd like to, but despite being gay, I don't have the knack for flower arranging," he said. He kissed Eliza's cheek and walked to the front door.

"Are you coming to dinner at Mom and Dad's tonight?"

Kit paused in the doorway. "No way."

"Why not? Your niece would love to see you. Do you know that you haven't seen Jennifer since her thirteenth-birthday party and she'll be fourteen soon?"

"You don't play fair, but I'm not coming. Mom and Dad managed to control themselves at *my* birthday party, but if I come to dinner, they'll bring up the whole marriage thing, and it'll turn into a great big ugly fight like it always does. The only way I'm going to dinner with the folks is if someone provides air support."

"I know they pick at you, but in their hearts, they just want you to be happy."

"Yeah, as long as it's with a wife and kids."

"We've been all through this. Sure they'd be shocked at first if you came out to them, but once they got over it and got used to the idea, they'd remember they love you just as you are."

"Maybe, but do you blame me for avoiding it as long as I can?"

"No, because I know how much it would hurt everyone involved. But pain goes away, and if you're going to come out, wouldn't it be better to do it on your own terms, rather than let them find out by accident?"

Kit opened the door for a woman approaching the entrance and slipped out in her wake. He'd had this conversation before, and he knew how it ended. He had two choices. He could please himself and feel like a selfish ingrate for the rest of his life, or he could please his parents and live a cruel lie for the rest of his life. Neither was appealing, and it was a decision he was going to postpone for as long as he was able. And if he spent a good deal of his free time trying to forget his problems, who could blame him?

Kit's phone rang as he was unlocking his car door. He slipped into the Ferrari as he answered. "Kit Britten speaking."

"I'm glad you're speaking, because I want to talk to you."

Kit recognized Romy's voice right away. "Romy O'Keefe, how are you?"

"I'm good. Are you missing your sunglasses? I found a pair in the office."

"So that's where they are." Kit left the parking structure and pulled onto the city street.

"They'll be here at the garage every day during business hours, which are eight to six."

"Where will they be the rest of the time?"

Romy chuckled and Kit's groin tightened in arousal. "You can pick them up whenever it's convenient for you," he said.

"It's convenient right now."

"I guess I'll see you soon, then."

"Give me about half an hour to get there."

"I'll be here," Romy said and hung up.

Kit put his phone down on the console and his foot down on the accelerator. It had taken Romy O'Keefe long enough to find the damned sunglasses, and Kit didn't want to waste any more time.

CHAPTER
THREE

KIT EASILY found his way back to the garage and parked in the small lot. Locking the car, he went to the office, but no one was there. He called Romy's name as he walked through the connecting door to the work area.

"Hi," Romy called out as he walked from the back of the shop. He pulled the cloth cap from his head and his glossy hair tumbled to his shoulders.

Kit instantly imagined the thick silky-looking strands sliding over his bare skin. Overwhelmed by the sudden sensory illusion, he couldn't reply as Romy came closer. His cheeks felt warm, and he was sure he was blushing.

"Your sunglasses are in the office," Romy said. "Follow me."

Romy walked past Kit, unzipping his coveralls to the waist and sliding his arms out of the sleeves. Kit followed like he'd been hypnotized, his gaze lingering on the lean muscles and smooth tanned skin of Romy's forearms. When Romy bent over to fetch something from under the counter, the cotton coveralls drew tight over his firm ass, and Kit swallowed hard as he was squeezed in the grip of desire.

"Here you go." Romy turned and held out his hand.

Kit stared at his sunglasses as though he'd never seen them before.

"These are yours, aren't they?" Romy asked.

Kit snapped out of his sensual trance. "Um, yeah. Those are mine." He took the sunglasses. "Thanks."

"No problem."

Romy and Kit looked at each other in silence for a moment, and then Romy spoke.

"I see you still have that sweet ride." The mechanic gestured toward the front window where the Ferrari was visible.

"Yeah." Kit glanced at the car. "Haven't had any more problems with it."

"Someday, I want to drive a car like that."

Kit blinked. This was an opportunity if he'd ever heard one. "How about today?" he said.

"Seriously?"

"Why not? It's insured. And I do owe you a favor."

Romy grinned. "Today, I close early."

Kit waited by the car while Romy changed. When Romy returned, he'd shed his coveralls and put on a pair of well-worn jeans and a rugby shirt, and he'd pulled his hair back into a ponytail. Kit got into the passenger seat and Romy slid in on the driver's side and closed the door. His left hand stroked the curve of the steering wheel as he put his right forefinger on the start button.

"Seat belt," Kit said.

"I was lost in the moment," Romy said as he buckled up. "Listen to that engine."

"You really like cars."

"Well, yeah, that's why I'm a mechanic. I can't afford my own Ferrari yet, but at least I can be around them sometimes." Romy made a wry face. "Stupid, right?"

"No! I like how you... *appreciate* this car. You deserve it more than I do."

"Where should we go?" Romy asked as he reached for the gearshift. When Kit didn't answer right away, Romy turned to look at him.

Kit dragged his gaze from Romy's fingers wrapped around the gearshift knob and met Romy's eyes. "What?" Kit said.

Romy raised his eyebrows. "Where do you want to go?"

"You have the wheel, and I have nowhere I have to be. Just drive until you get tired of it."

"You might regret saying that."

Romy revved the engine a little before shifting. The sleek car leapt forward and Romy continued to shift up until they were running wide open down the street. At the corner, he tapped the brake, downshifted, and let the rear end drift around the right-angle turn to the music of Kit's delighted laughter. Hitting the gas again, he slalomed through traffic to the freeway ramp. Not until they'd merged onto the high-speed throughway to Galveston did Romy take his eyes off the road and glance at his passenger.

"That was fun," Kit said.

A relieved smile lit Romy's face. Kit wasn't at all upset about the way his car had been handled. In fact, Kit seemed quite happy about the whole experience.

"So where are we going?" Kit asked.

"I'd like to open her up on the freeway, and if you're hungry, there's a place out this way that has great food. At least they did the last time I was there."

Kit realized abruptly that he was indeed very hungry. "Let's go," he said.

For the next half hour, Romy and Kit enjoyed the ride while getting better acquainted. By the time they arrived at the little restaurant near the Gulf, they were well on the way to becoming friends. As they entered, Kit laughed at one of Romy's deadpan remarks and got a smile from the woman who hurried to greet them.

"What brings two such handsome young men to my little restaurant?" she said as she seated her guests.

"We heard the food was good and the owner was beautiful," Romy answered.

"Don't bother flirting with me. I'm old enough to be your mother."

Kit watched Romy charm the lady, seeing another side of the quiet mechanic. "You promised me good food," Kit said, breaking into the polite banter.

"Let me get some menus," the woman said.

"That's okay," Kit said. "Just bring me your favorite pasta dish." He paused. "And a bottle of house wine." He looked at Romy. "You'll drive back, right?"

"I'll be your chauffeur for as long as you need one."

The dinner conversation centered around favorite movies and songs with sidetracks into a hundred related areas, and both men found themselves pleasantly entertained. When Romy insisted on paying for dinner, Kit gave in graciously but insisted on leaving the tip. On the ride home, Kit wanted the windows down, making it difficult to talk without shouting, and so they rode in silence. Romy piloted the car through the return route with nonchalant skill as Kit played with the slipstream. Each stole surreptitious glances at the other, taking screenshots to be filed away to moon over later in private.

"I'll bet my hair's a mess," Kit said, showing no inclination to get out of the car after Romy parked at the garage.

"It's sexy, windblown, and carefree," Romy said in a cheesy TV announcer's voice.

There was just enough alcohol in Kit's system to loosen the small amount of control he had over his tongue. "You think I'm sexy?" he purred. "You want to kiss me? And touch me all over? You naughty boy. I'm not that type!"

Romy grinned, his teeth a gleaming half-moon under the parking-lot lights. "You're a little crazy, aren't you, Kit Britten?"

Kit backpedaled quickly. "I confess. I can't be serious for more than ten minutes, but I don't mean any offense by it."

"I'm not offended. In fact—" Romy cleared his throat. "Look, I know we met by pure chance, so I don't want to make it more than it is, but…. I just want to say I enjoy your company. And thanks for letting me drive your car. This might be just another day in the Lone Star State for you, but for me, it was pretty special."

"It was special for me too," Kit said quickly—maybe a little too quickly, he thought. "I don't have a lot of friends my age," he added even more quickly. "It's fun to just hang out sometimes."

"You sound a little uncomfortable. I'm sorry if I pushed things."

"No, no, no, no, no!" Kit took a breath. "It's not like that at all. I was afraid you'd think I was a total girl if I said what I really wanted to."

"Which was?"

"Oh come on. You don't expect me to say it *now*, do you?"

"Okay. As long as I didn't offend you."

"You didn't. At all."

"You think maybe we should do this again?"

"Yes. We definitely should." Relief made Kit feel abruptly shaky, and he covered his reaction by getting out of the car. "Call me sometime," he said as he walked around to the driver's side.

"I've still got your card," Romy said. He didn't add that the card was enshrined on his dresser, but it was. It had pride of place among the small items that Romy had saved for sentimental reasons.

"I'm serious. Call me," Kit said as he got into the car.

"Count on it."

Kiss me. Kit willed Romy to lean in the open door and kiss him. When his attempt at mind control failed, Kit spoke. "I'm not always crazy," he said.

"Thanks for the warning. Good night, Kit Britten."

"Good night," Kit said as he started the car. He tried to think of a reason to stay longer, but it looked as though the evening was really at an end. "Call me," he said again.

No, that didn't sound desperate at all, Kit scolded himself as he drove away. His phone rang before he got to the corner.

"Are you busy Friday?"

Kit shivered as Romy's vibrant voice stroked his ear. "No," he said, without even thinking about it. "What have you got in mind?"

"There's a place not far from the garage where the music is hot and the drinks are ice-cold. Sound tempting?"

"You could make a living on the radio," Kit said. "You've really got the voice for it."

Romy laughed. "My old boss used to say that. You want directions to the bar, or do you want to meet me here on Friday around eight?"

"I'll meet you at the garage, and we can go together."

"Sounds like a plan," Romy said. "Good night again."

"Good night again." Kit laughed softly as he hung up and set the phone aside. He had something to look forward to. Life was good.

Romy went around the back of the garage to the travel trailer he called home. It looked like something good was finally happening in his life after a long string of setbacks. As he got ready for bed, he cautioned himself to take things slowly. *Don't be too clingy,* he thought as he lay down. *And don't show weakness. Above all, don't dive in headfirst before you check for water in the pool.*

FOUR

ELIZA SWATTED the back of Kit's head.

"What was that for?" he asked as he rearranged his hair in the dressing-room mirror.

"You were bouncing."

"Bouncing?"

"Yes, bouncing and making it impossible for me to fix this hem."

"Sorry." Kit held himself in stillness as Eliza plied her needle on the bottom of his pullover shirt.

"If you didn't pull on the hem all the time, this wouldn't happen," she said as she tied off the knot and sat back. She put away her sewing kit and took a look at Kit as he stood still for her inspection. "I like you in that shirt," she said. "It's casual, but the shape accents your body well."

"You're making me blush."

Eliza snorted. "Don't pretend to be embarrassed by a compliment, or why spend all that time working out?"

"I like being in good shape. It's healthy."

"And it's just a coincidence that your healthy shape is attractive?"

"Tease me all you want. You can't ruin my good mood."

"I wasn't trying to. So what's making you bounce today?"

"I have a date tonight." Kit paused. "Sort of. I'm meeting a new friend for drinks."

Eliza gave him a long look. "You're being careful, right? And honest?"

Kit nodded. "I'm going to tell him I'm gay, I swear."

"Good. It's the right thing to do if you're going to keep seeing him."

"I know." Kit looked around the closed shop. "Anything else I can do for you?"

"You can go and have fun." Eliza smoothed the shoulders of Kit's shirt. "And always remember I'm here if you need to talk."

"You're sure I look all right?" Kit held his arms out from his sides and pivoted slowly on his heel. The white pullover hugged the contours of his chest and abdomen and the bleach-splashed jeans looked painted onto his long legs.

Eliza tugged on the dark-red bangs that shadowed Kit's forehead. "Go to the mirror if you want to see what perfection looks like, but don't fish for compliments from me."

"I just don't want to seem like I'm trying too hard."

"I see, you don't want to look like you're trying, but if he turns out to be gay, you want to hit him like a sex bomb. Is that about right?"

"Sex bomb? Where did you hear that phrase?"

"It was in some movie I watched with Katherine."

Kit shook his head. "That girl is a bad influence," he joked.

"Don't talk about your sister like that." Eliza swatted Kit's bottom. "Go!"

Though he didn't want to look overeager, Kit was at O'Keefe's Garage fifteen minutes early. Romy was waiting with the roll-up door open.

"The bar's close enough to walk to," Romy said. "Go ahead and pull your car inside. Can't be too careful around here."

After rolling down the door, Romy locked up, giving Kit a chance to admire him in a pair of skinny black jeans and a striped oxford shirt. Romy's hair was loose, falling around his face in shining waves that Kit found near irresistible. More than once he had to conquer the impulse to reach out and stroke Romy's hair.

"Ready?" Romy asked, pocketing his keys.

Kit nodded and they began walking.

"I seem to remember warning you about how tough this neighborhood is," Romy said.

"I seem to remember you telling me I was going to get my ass kicked."

"Well, you don't have to worry about the bar we're going to. It's my regular hangout and everyone there is cool."

"I'm sure you'll defend my honor if it comes to that."

Romy chuckled. "You can count on it," he said.

"Are you sure? Maybe I should see your lance first."

"Lunatic." Romy shook his head, but he was grinning. "And anyway, I don't want to scare you, or make you feel inadequate, or anything."

Kit laughed. "I'm not afraid," he said.

"I kind of got that idea about you. You're not afraid of much, are you?"

"There are one or two things, but mostly, I don't see the point in being scared. I just move ahead, and if I make a mistake, I try to correct it, but at least I didn't sit around worrying."

"That's your philosophy, is it?"

"I guess."

Romy was silent for a moment before he spoke. "I like it," he said.

Warmth bloomed at Kit's core and spread outward to every fiber of his being. "Then I'll consider having it carved in stone," he said as casually as he could manage.

Romy smacked Kit on the back. "Don't be a jerk," he said.

Kit's skin tingled where Romy had touched him, and he wondered if his glow was visible. "I was serious!" he exclaimed. He loved this bantering stage of courtship and was happy to find that Romy enjoyed it too.

"You're really good at the innocent look, but I'm not buying it." Romy slowed and turned down a narrow alleyway.

"The club's down here?" Kit asked as he followed. "I didn't see a sign."

"It's kind of a private club."

"This is more interesting by the minute," Kit said happily.

A short while later, they walked down a flight of concrete steps and entered a large basement. The lighting was discreet, but Kit could see a couple of dozen tables in a semicircle around a stage. His visual tour ended there when he got a look at the singer. His ears had already informed him that someone of exceptional talent was performing, and now he could see that the singer's looks matched the voice. The young man holding the microphone had the body of a gymnast and the face of an impish angel under a spiky mop of hair as blue-white as 1% milk. Behind him was a standard lineup of guitar, bass, keyboard, and drums, but there was nothing standard about their stage presence.

"I'm impressed already," Kit said.

Romy smiled. "I had a suspicion you might like it. Want to sit at the bar or at a table?"

"Table, if possible. I want to watch the show."

Romy and Kit sat down at a small table to the right of the stage. As soon as the song was over, a waiter arrived to take drink orders. It was obvious from the waiter's manner that Romy was a regular and well-regarded customer and Kit approved. He believed you could tell a lot about a person by the way they treated the wait staff.

The band launched into another song and Romy and Kit gave the performance their full attention. The singer had put the microphone on a stand and was performing a very athletic pole dance with it. Kit was rather impressed by the performer's fluid hip thrusts. When the drinks arrived, Kit finished his in a few large gulps.

"Are you in a hurry?" Romy asked as he signaled the waiter to return.

"I just felt hot all of a sudden." Kit ordered another cocktail. "I may have to drink a lot."

"Fine with me. I'm walking home," Romy said.

On stage, the singer was thanking the audience and telling them that ImproVice would be back after a short break. To Kit's astonishment, he then leaped from the stage to throw his arms around Romy from behind. Kissing Romy soundly on the cheek, the singer turned his smoky gaze on Kit.

"Kit Britten," Romy said. "Meet Joplin Fraser."

"Hi," Kit said. "Pleased to meet you. You're an amazing performer."

"Thanks," Joplin said, leaning on Romy's shoulder. "Rome brought you here, so you must be all right. Welcome to Stardust."

"Stardust?" Kit repeated.

"That's the name of the club," Romy said.

"Blame him." Joplin bumped Romy's shoulder. "He named it."

"It's my favorite song." Romy shrugged.

"I don't know it," Kit said.

"Then allow me to introduce you," Joplin said. Leaping back onto the stage with the agility and grace of the average panther, Joplin took up the microphone and crooned an a capella version of the old classic.

"That's beautiful," Kit said. "I've heard the melody before, in a movie, I think, but I've never heard the words. It's kind of sad, isn't it?"

"Kind of," Romy said returning Joplin's wave.

Kit watched Joplin walk over to the bar. "He's really something," he said, squelching his jealousy. *So what if that hypersexy, supertalented gorgeous man was all touchy-feely with Romy. That didn't have to mean anything. There was no point in wondering if they'd been lovers, or in picturing them going at it.* But Kit did, of course.

"He's a fireball," Romy answered. "And I believe he'll make it out of the neighborhood someday with a fat recording contract."

"He's got what it takes, that's for sure." Kit raised his glass. "To Joplin," he said and took a drink. "How long have you been friends?"

"He's the first person that was nice to me when my family moved here. We've known each other since we were ten."

"So you're *really* good friends."

"I like to think so. We don't hang out like we did when we were in school though. He's working hard to be a rock star, which doesn't leave much time for socializing with anyone but the other guys in the band."

"That's too bad," Kit replied, secretly pleased that Romy wasn't spending a lot of time with the divinely rumped Joplin. "Is this the only bar you go to?"

"It's close and I know the owners. Did you want to go somewhere else?"

"No, I was just wondering if you knew any other good places."

"Not really. How about you?"

"Do you know a place called Deep Indigo?"

Romy hooked his arm over the back of his chair and faced Kit directly. "Is that really what you want to ask me?"

Flustered, Kit took another drink.

"Indigo's a known gay bar, isn't it?" Romy said. "Are you asking if I'm gay?" He took hold of Kit's wrist as Kit started to raise his glass. "Just ask," he said.

"Well… are you?"

"Does it make a difference?"

"Yes. A big one."

"Are you going to decide you can't be my friend if I turn out to be gay?"

"I'm hoping like hell that you're gay."

Romy smiled. "I am if you are," he drawled.

CHAPTER
FIVE

KIT CLOSED his eyes for a second and heard his sister telling him to be brave. "I'm gay," he said and finished off his drink.

"Me, too," Romy said. "Aren't you glad that's out of the way?"

"I don't know what I would've done if you'd said no," Kit said.

"But I didn't. So what now?"

"I know what I'd like to do. I've been fantasizing about it since the first second I saw you."

"Does it involve being horizontal?"

"Eventually."

Romy leaned over the table. "Look, I like you a lot, but I have to know up front. Am I getting in over my head with you?"

"In what way?"

"Like are you some sort of sex addict working your way through the Houston phone book?"

Kit gaped at Romy. "No! Are you?"

"Not even close. I've never even had anyone you could call a boyfriend."

"Are you a virgin?" Kit asked, half in hope, half in fear.

"It's not that bad." Romy smiled. "I've fooled around here and there, but up until about six months ago, I lived at home with my mom and little brother Ricardo. Cardo's ten years younger, and he and I shared a bedroom, so I couldn't exactly—"

"But you have your own place now, right?" Kit interrupted.

"Yeah, but it's not what I'd call deluxe accommodations."

"I'm not a snob."

"I'm getting that impression." Romy signaled the waiter. "Why don't we just relax and have a good time and see what happens?"

"Sounds good, as long as you know you'll probably have to defend your honor against me at some point in the evening."

"I look forward to it."

Joplin's band returned to the stage and filled the space with music, leaving no room for conversation. Kit and Romy enjoyed the show, making frequent eye contact, and occasionally touching hands under the guise of making toasts. When Joplin came over to the table again, Kit wasn't nearly as intimidated by the singer who exuded a sweet, hot sexiness Kit frankly envied. He was so honest about it, he complimented Joplin on his appeal.

"That's funny," Joplin said. "I was going to say the same thing to you. You look young and innocent, but you've got that gleam in your eye."

"There's no need to mock me," Kit said.

"Tell him I'm serious." Joplin poked Romy.

"Joplin doesn't fuck around," Romy said and got poked again. Hard. "Ow!"

"Thanks for the compliment, then," Kit told Joplin. "But if I could move my hips like yours, I'd just fuck around all night... and all day."

Joplin started laughing and couldn't stop.

"Now you've done it," Romy told Kit. "Now he'll be useless."

"It wasn't even that funny," Kit said in his defense.

"Hey, who broke Joplin?" The band's tall guitarist loomed over the table.

"He'll be fine, Koda," Romy said. "Why don't you take him to the dressing room? You and Zippy and Mark and The Heater can give him a good cuddle."

Koda lifted Joplin. "I like the way you think," he said as he walked away with a hiccupping Joplin over his shoulder.

"Is it wrong that I'm picturing a gang bang?" Kit asked.

"Maybe, but it's accurate."

"Hmmm, is it wrong that I'm kind of turned on?"

"I think you need some fresh air." Romy stood up. "Want to go for a walk?"

Kit got to his feet and led the way to the door. "Wait. I didn't pay," he said.

"I have a tab," Romy said.

"You shouldn't have to pay for all the drinks. It's not like this is a date or anything."

"I'd like it if it was." Romy put a hand under Kit's elbow as they went up the steps to street level.

Kit stopped on the top step with the moon behind his head, haloing his hair and putting his face in shadow. "You want to date me?"

"If it's not asking too much." Romy couldn't see Kit's expression, but he kept his tone casual, not letting on how much Kit's answer meant to him.

"That's *so* cool!" Kit said. "Because I really want to keep going out with you."

"I'm glad you like the idea." Romy joined Kit on the sidewalk. "I know I can't wine you and dine you in the style you're accustomed to, but I'll do my best to show you a good time."

"I can't wait!"

"You're bouncing," Romy said.

"Really?"

"Yeah." Romy tilted his head to the side. "It's cute."

"I'm cute!" Kit crowed to the streetlight.

Romy hooked his arm through Kit's and led him gently down the street. "You're very cute," he said. "And a little drunk."

"Don't exaggerate. I'm a lot drunk. Wait a second. What's the opposite of exaggerate?"

"I don't know."

"Is that an understatement?"

Romy grinned. "You're good-looking *and* smart. I can't believe my luck."

"Me either."

"I mean I can hardly believe someone like you would go out with someone like me."

"Why wouldn't I?"

"Well, for one thing, there's a significant gap in our—"

"Don't finish that sentence," Kit said, as he stopped and put his forefinger against Romy's lips. "I know what you're going to say, and it's demeaning to you and insulting to me. So please don't say it." He let his hand trail down Romy's chin and neck, bumping over the prominent Adam's apple. "We're just two people, okay?"

Romy took hold of Kit's wrist, holding Kit's hand in place as he pressed his lips to the pad of Kit's finger in a kiss of acquiescence. Kit smiled, and Romy touched the tip of his tongue to the same spot in an almost subliminal caress. Kit's eyelids drifted down and his lips parted on a soft gasp.

"Wow," Kit breathed. "I can't believe how turned on I am right now."

"I want you so much.... I can't even think of a word for how much I want you."

Kit's eyes were locked on Romy's mouth and his pink tongue swiped at his lower lip in an act of sympathetic magic. "What should we do about this?" he asked softly.

"We should get off the street." Romy took Kit's arm again and started walking.

"Am I being too forward? Everyone tells me I'm too forward. You can tell me to slow down if—"

"Relax," Romy said, patting Kit's hand. "I like everything about you, so if you're worried about me liking you, just be yourself."

"I can't help thinking you're too good to be true." Kit stopped. "What if it turns out you're my long-lost half brother?"

"That's a little melodramatic, isn't it?"

"And you fell for it!" Kit's delighted laughter pealed out as he hung on Romy's arm.

"You got me," Romy admitted.

"I watch too many soap operas," Kit said.

"What's your favorite?"

"As if you'd know anything about it."

"When I'm working, I leave the television on. I don't see much of it, but I hear everything."

"I don't want to talk about it."

"Why not?"

"It's embarrassing."

"Why?"

"Why? Are you kidding? They're soap operas."

"They're serialized dramas," Romy said. "There now, don't you feel better about it already?"

"Serialized dramas, you say? I like that. I just wish they weren't so easy to get addicted to."

"Let me guess, you like the ones where the lead character's honor won't let him be with the person he loves."

"Those are my favorites, especially if the actor is handsome," Kit confessed as they turned down the street the garage was on. "I know they're sappy, but I love them."

Romy leaned close and spoke in Kit's ear as though confiding a secret. "So do I," he said, his breath warm against Kit's skin.

Kit turned to meet Romy's gaze, his lust-blind eyes glazed by the purple-white streetlight. His pulse was pounding so hard he could feel it in his throat. Time slowed as Romy's eyes locked on Kit's and their souls trembled on the threshold of a great awakening. A car passed by and its headlights swept over the couple on the sidewalk, jarring them from their trance. Someone yelled out of the vehicle's window in a harsh, jeering blast of indistinguishable words.

"Come on," Romy said. "Let's get inside."

CHAPTER
SIX

"MAKE YOURSELF at home," Romy said as he held the trailer door open for Kit.

Kit was admiring the sleek lines of the aerodynamic aluminum teardrop Romy lived in. "It's cute," he said as he stepped inside.

"There isn't a lot of room, but it'll work for now." Romy went into the tiny kitchen area and filled the coffee machine with fresh water. "Coffee?" he offered.

Kit turned from inspecting a small shelf of books. "Yeah, thanks," he said as he came to lean on the counter that separated the kitchen from the living/dining area.

Romy pointed over his shoulder with his thumb. "Bathroom's in the hall," he said as he measured coffee into the paper filter.

"And the bedroom's at the end?"

"Yep." Romy pushed the start button on the coffeemaker. "This'll just take a minute," he said as he reached down a couple of cups from an overhead cabinet.

"I'm in no hurry. Too drunk to drive right now."

"I do admire your capacity for alcohol. Most people would be blind, staggering drunk if they drank as much as you did."

"It's a gift." Kit smiled. "I notice you drank just as much and you're not even slurring your words."

"Maybe we really are half brothers."

Kit threw his head back and laughed, promptly banging his skull on the bottom of the kitchen cabinet. Romy looked shocked for half a second, with round eyes and a dropped jaw, and then he burst into laughter.

"I'm sorry," Romy said breathlessly. "But I couldn't help it. The look on your face!"

Kit rubbed the top of his head. "It's okay. I would've laughed if it happened to you."

"I'm used to living in close quarters. You learn to watch your head and keep your elbows tucked in. No large motions."

"I'm all over the place."

"You *are* kind of larger than life."

"Yeah, I know. I'm too loud, too colorful, too—"

"Who says so?"

"My parents. My teachers. My therapist."

"You have a therapist?"

Kit watched Romy pour the coffee. "Not anymore. That was when I was a kid. I was hyperactive, they said."

"Milk? Sugar?"

"Both, please."

"Hyperactive, huh?" Romy said as he put a small carton of milk and a sugar shaker on the counter. "You've got a lot of energy, but that's not necessarily a bad thing."

"The therapist put me on drugs. I had such a bad reaction they never tried that again."

"So how did they ever cure you and produce this stunning example of reserved humanity that stands before me now?"

Kit chuckled as he stirred his coffee. "My mom sent me to my sisters' comportment coach."

"Excuse the fuck out of me, but what the hell's a comportment coach?"

"Someone who teaches you how to behave in public. The same lady polished up my sisters before their debutante balls."

"No shit. So they teach you things like etiquette?"

"Yeah, things like that." Kit sipped his coffee. "Let's talk about you. All I really know is that you have a mom and a little brother, a great sense of humor, and you like rhythm and blues and scary sci-fi movies."

"I'm not that interesting."

"I see a chessboard over there."

"I play myself sometimes, just for grins."

"My dad taught me the basic moves, but I never got into it." Kit paused. "Will you play with me someday?"

Romy took a drink of his black coffee. "Someday."

Kit broke the brief silence. "Why is this moment always so weird?"

"You mean the one where we're deciding whether we're going to sleep together?"

"No, I decided that a long time ago. This is the moment where we know we're going to sleep together and we're just waiting for the right signal."

"I was having a different moment, I guess." Romy grinned at Kit's change of expression. "Got you back," he said.

Kit composed himself. "Yes, you did get me back. I can see I'm playing a master."

"I had a little brother to practice on."

"And all I had were five older sisters who were off-limits for pranks."

"Considering your handicap, you're a very impressive player."

"And you're stalling." Kit held up his cup as though offering it as evidence.

"You're right." Romy leaned his elbows on the counter, bracketing his coffee with his forearms. "But hear me out. I don't want this to be all about the sex. I really like you. I like just being with you, seeing you, and hearing your voice. I can't explain why, but it makes me feel good. So I want to keep seeing you."

"I feel the same way."

"Call me crazy, but I'm afraid if we rush to bed—"

"You're crazy," Kit interrupted. "But I understand how it is when you have a feeling about something. We don't have to have sex tonight." He paused. "Even though I know it would be the best sex in the history of fucking."

"You're amazing. Did you know that? Have I mentioned it?"

"Feel free to mention it as often as you like."

"How about tomorrow night? We could have dinner and watch a DVD or something."

"I'd love that." Kit grinned.

Romy felt Kit's happiness like a beam of sunlight shining just on him. "You could call me when you get off work."

"I might not be able to wait that long."

"I know how you feel, but I can't take off early tomorrow." Romy came around the counter. "Don't pout." He pulled Kit into his arms, hugging him tightly.

Kit freed his arms and wrapped them around Romy. With a happy sigh, he snuggled closer, taking in Romy's scent with each breath. He had the feeling he was getting the hug normally reserved for Romy's little brother, but he was content for the moment to be held in an embrace that embodied comfort and protection. "I should probably go soon and let you get some sleep," Kit said to make things easier on Romy.

"Do you want to go?"

"No, I want to stay like this forever, but I know you have to get up early."

"True. Just a few more minutes, okay? It feels so good holding you."

Kit drew back just far enough to look into Romy's eyes. The tip of his nose brushed Romy's cheek and then the softness of Romy's lips covered his. He closed his eyes and pressed his lips to Romy's, moving them in a silent request for more, as he slid his fingers into Romy's hair. Romy's hand came up to cradle the back of Kit's head as Kit pulled away slightly. Their eyes met again, just a glance, an acknowledgment that this was real, was truly happening to them, and then their mouths came together again in a deeper kiss that was less gentle but just as sweet. Passion flared and they pressed closer, mouths working, muscles straining, yearning to merge in every way possible.

Romy broke the kiss. "Shh" he whispered into Kit's mouth. "We should stop now."

Kit made a disappointed noise. "I don't want to, but I'll try to be an adult about it."

Romy glanced down. "That feels amazing, but seriously, we should stop."

"What?"

"Are you unaware that you're rubbing your hard-on against mine?"

"Oops." Kit made a sheepish face.

Romy kissed Kit and let him go. "Go home now so I can miss you," he said.

Kit took out his phone. "It's only one," he said.

"And I open shop at six."

"Right." Kit leaned to kiss Romy. "I'll call you," he said as his phone chimed to let him know he had a text. He looked at the text and then up at Romy who was taking his hand out of his pocket. "How'd you do that?" Kit asked.

Romy wiggled his fingers. "I have nimble digits." He smirked.

Kit bit his lip in a wistful expression. "You're not making it easy for me to leave."

"One more hug," Romy said. His breath went out in a rush as Kit slammed into his chest and squeezed him tight. Romy returned the embrace with equal passion, holding Kit close. "This is good," he murmured in Kit's ear.

They separated, long before either wanted to, and parted with another kiss. Kit forced himself out the door and got in his car. He waved to Romy and then drove away. Only the knowledge that he'd see Romy tomorrow made it bearable.

So much for being careful. All right, so he *had* fallen head over heels for Romy O'Keefe. Kit looked down at the text that was still displayed on his phone. A slow smile spread over his face. There was evidence to suggest that Romy felt the same way about him. He shifted into fourth and reached down to give his crotch a squeeze. Now the question was: could he make it home to jerk off in the shower, or was he going to have to pull off the road as soon as he found a good spot?

Romy rinsed the coffee carafe, washed the cups, dried them, and put them away. He washed his face, brushed his teeth, and got undressed. The whole time, he was thinking about Kit and kisses sweeter than cotton candy, more intoxicating than a tanker truck of tequila. He lay naked on his bed and let his fingers wander up and down his torso until it seemed like their idea when he finally took hold of his hard-on. With vivid images of Kit occupying his imagination, he came quickly and fell asleep with his cock cradled in his underwear-gloved hand.

CHAPTER

SEVEN

KIT'S PHONE rang while he was at lunch. He glanced at the number and then apologized to the others at the table. Walking quickly, he went to the restaurant's foyer and called Romy.

"Sorry I couldn't pick up," he said when Romy answered. "I'm at a business lunch."

"We can talk later."

"No, it's fine."

"It's not important. I just wanted to hear your voice."

Kit smiled. "We're still on for tonight, right?"

"Absolutely, but do you mind if we stay in. I didn't get much sleep last night."

"Me either and it's all your fault."

"We can share the blame."

"Why don't you come to my place? I can cook, or we can order in."

"Sure. Just give me the address."

"I'll text it to you." Kit sighed. "I wish I was with you instead of here."

"You sound bored."

"I am. It's a really great restaurant, but I'm eating with my boss, the property manager, and the accounts manager. I don't even understand what they're saying half the time."

"I'll bet that isn't true. Whenever you say something business related to me, you sound like you know what you're talking about."

"You're making me blush," Kit said in a pleased voice. "How soon can I see you?"

"I close at six. How far is it to your place?"

"About a half hour."

"Okay. So counting a shower and travel time—"

"You can shower here."

Romy chuckled, pleased by Kit's eagerness to see him. "I'll take a quick shower. Are you sure you don't want to go out? I could make the effort for you."

"It's fine. I've already got a movie picked out. Just come over as soon as you can."

"I will. A customer just came in so... 'bye for now."

Kit said good-bye and hung up. He barely felt the marble floor under his boots as he floated back to the table.

"Earth to Kit," said Kit's sister Julianne, an accountant who kept the books for Eliza's shop. "Check it out, girls."

"Kissy's been like that all day, Jules. All week, really," Eliza said as she turned to the woman on her right. "What do you think, Jackie?"

Jacqueline Britten-Baines was another of Kit's sisters. She had a real estate broker's license and managed the boutique property for Eliza. "I love seeing him happy, but I think if he smiles like that around Mom, she's going to assume he's in love and demand he bring the girl to dinner." She smiled at Kit as he sat down. "But there isn't a girl, is there?"

"What are we talking about?" Kit asked.

"Your new boyfriend," Eliza said.

"I guess there's no such thing as privacy in this family," Kit said.

"Not that I've noticed," Jules muttered.

"I don't want to talk about him," Kit said.

"You *don't* want to talk about him?" Jackie glanced at her sisters. "It must be serious."

"We've barely known each other a week. Can you just let it drop?"

"Not likely," Jules said. "Your sisters are all either married, engaged, or terminally undatable." She glanced at Jackie and then back at Kit. "So all we have to talk about is *your* love life."

"At least tell us if he's nice," Jackie said.

"I want to know if he's handsome!" Jules said.

"And gay," Eliza added pointedly.

Kit played with his napkin as he answered. "He's gay. He's beautiful. And he's the nicest man I've ever met."

"That sounds like a good start," Jackie said.

"Does he make you laugh?" Jules asked.

Kit nodded. "He's hilarious when he wants to be."

"Then I'm happy for you," Jackie said.

"And it's about time," Jules said. "Two years is long enough to get over—"

"Hush," Eliza said. "No need to bring up the past right now."

"Right," Jackie said, raising her wineglass in a toast. "To a happy future for our brother, our families, and our business."

Everyone touched glasses and took a sip of wine.

"Now, I'm sorry to bring it up," Eliza said. "But Kit, when are you going to tell Mom and Dad you're gay? You're twenty-four. You're out of college, you have a job and your own place. They're not going to be put off for much longer."

"You're going to have to tell them something," Jules said.

Jackie nodded. "You can't avoid them forever."

"I can try," Kit said.

"You have until next Saturday," Eliza said. "Everyone will be at my barbeque, I'm assuming."

Kit opened his mouth to speak but closed it again when Eliza looked at him.

"Bring your boyfriend if you want to," Eliza said. "Even if you don't come out before then, it would be nice to have him there as your friend."

"I'll ask him," Kit said.

"Good," Eliza said. "If you like him so much, I'm sure we will too."

"If you're through planning my life for the moment, I need to go."

Eliza looked at her phone. "It's barely four thirty and we've only opened one bottle of wine. What's your hurry?"

"If you must know, I have a date," Kit said. "And I don't have time to sit around talking about it."

"Why not?" Jules asked.

"Because he's coming to my place. I need to do a little tidying."

"Come on, Kissy." Jackie rolled her eyes. "Your place looks like a magazine photo."

"It's always perfect," Jules said.

"Because he's never there," Eliza added. "I think we're seeing more evidence that our baby brother is serious about this guy."

"I just want to make sure it looks like the right kind of magazine photo." Kit stood, dropping his napkin on his chair. "If you let me go, I promise to text you all about it tomorrow."

"Go and have a good time," Eliza said.

Kit said good-bye to his sisters and left the restaurant. For the next hour and a half, he shopped. Struck by the sudden fear that none of his clothes were right for a stay-at-home date, he bought several sweat suits. As usual, a few other items caught his eye and he ended up with bags from more than a few shops. Deciding he didn't have time to stop at his local gourmet food store, he called and placed an order for delivery. Just before he reached his apartment building, he stopped at a liquor store and picked out three bottles of wine. Mr. Martinez, the doorman of Kit's building, was favored with a big smile as he held the door open. Humming happily, Kit took the elevator to his ninth-floor apartment. Once inside he dropped the shopping bags on his bed and went into the kitchen.

"Okay," he said after a few minutes of inspecting the refrigerator. "I think we're all set, as long as the delivery isn't la—" Kit smiled as his intercom chimed. He went over and pressed the push-to-talk button. "Delivery for me?" he asked cheerfully.

After the delivery boy had dropped off the groceries, Kit unpacked the box. Some items went into the refrigerator, while Kit placed others on the counter. He reached a set of serving dishes down from an overhead cabinet and set out wineglasses. Satisfied that things were in order, Kit went to the bedroom.

His shower was a quick one, but the soapy water flowing over his bare skin heightened his already sensuous mood. He looked forward to sharing the tastes of good food and wine with Romy. He looked forward to sharing his favorite movie with Romy. And he very much looked forward to touching Romy again. He remembered the silky texture of Romy's hair and skin, the hardness of Romy's muscles, the roughness of the five-o'clock shadow, and he wanted to feel them all again on his way to uncharted territory.

Kit dried off, enjoying the brush of the towel against his skin as he walked into the bedroom. After considering his choices, he put on black track pants over a pair of skimpy black briefs. The soft pants and the T-shirt draped his physique in a flattering way that didn't put it on display, and the snug briefs bundled his junk into a nice, discreet package. And it was very comfortable without looking sloppy.

It was also the polar opposite of the way Kit usually dressed for a date. *Be brave*, he reminded himself. *You don't have to dazzle the guy with your bling. Just be you.*

Kit's phone rang, and he snatched it up off the bed. "Where are you?" he said as he answered.

CHAPTER
EIGHT

"I'M IN front of your apartment building," Romy said. "What's the procedure?"

"I'll call down and the doorman will let you in. Take the elevator to the ninth floor. There are only four apartments. I'm in 904, the farthest from the elevator." Kit said good-bye, called down to the lobby, and went into the kitchen to uncork the bottle of pinot noir. He put out a selection of cheeses, crackers, and jams, and ran to the bathroom. After a look in the mirror, he used his blow-dryer, brushed out his hair, and hurried back to the kitchen. Taking a cast-iron pot from the bottom shelf of the big fridge, he put it on the stove and turned on the burner. He looked around and what he saw pleased him, so he poured a mouthful of wine into one of the glasses and brought it to his nose. Kit inhaled deeply just as his doorbell rang. A smile curved his lips as he set the glass down and went to the door.

"Hi, it's me," Romy said as the door swung open.

Kit just stood there for a moment silently taking in the fact that Romy was right in front of him. Romy wore a perfectly ordinary white T-shirt and gray sweatshirt with a hole in the sleeve over worn jeans, and he had more style than any model Kit had ever dated. Romy's face was scrubbed shiny-clean and his thick hair was still damp from the shower, and he was still a thousand times more handsome than any of the aforementioned models. He had more grace, more wit, and more charm than anyone Kit had ever known. And each time Kit saw him, the effect deepened, and Kit fell further in love.

"I brought these," Romy said. He held out a small bouquet of chocolate flowers. "I know how silly it is, but—"

"I love them!" Kit took the chocolates. "Come in."

Romy walked in and looked around at the living room. "Nice," he said.

Kit shrugged. "My mom hired a designer to work with me when I moved in here. It's not exactly what most people would consider homey, but...."

"It looks like something you'd see in an expensive magazine. Just needs a bored-looking blonde about as big around as a soda straw lounging on that suede sofa."

Kit chuckled. "Yeah, I've heard that, just not in so many words. So, are you hungry? I've got snacks."

Romy followed Kit into the kitchen. "This is almost as big as my whole house," he said.

"Try this," Kit said, handing Romy a glass of wine.

Romy sipped. "Nice. I guess. I don't know much about wine."

"Me either. I buy what the guy at the wine store tells me to buy. Anyway, it's supposed to be good with this cheese." Kit spread some soft cheese on a cracker and offered it to Romy.

Romy leaned forward and ate it from Kit's fingers. He lifted his eyebrows in appreciation as he crunched, swallowed, and took a drink of the wine. "Very nice."

Kit recovered from the sensation of Romy's lips against his fingers and managed to make words come out of his mouth. "I'm glad you like it. I want you to like everything tonight."

"You're off to a great start."

"Thanks. I'll try to relax and not drive you crazy."

"You do whatever makes you happy. It's your house."

"Well, let's see. I have my infamous diablo stew warming up on the stove, which takes care of dinner. So for now, I'd like to sit on the couch with you and drink this wine." Kit picked up the cheese board. "Would you mind bringing the bottle?"

Kit and Romy settled on the large sofa with the snacks on the agate-topped table in front of them.

"If I saw this place in a magazine, I'd think it belonged to a world-class player," Romy said.

"Don't be silly," Kit said. "I barely made the nationals."

"But admit it, it's designed to seduce."

"Okay, you caught me. I had planned to overwhelm you with my lavish crib so I could get you drunk and take advantage of you."

"Just as I feared." Romy finished his wine in two long swallows and held out the glass.

Kit chuckled as he poured more wine for Romy. He took a sip from his glass at the same time Romy took a drink. Their eyes met and they smiled just because they felt happy to be sharing this moment. They lowered their glasses and reached for a piece of cheese at the same time. Their hands bumped and their eyes met again. And they smiled again.

"Go ahead," Kit said. "You're my guest."

"How did your lunch go after I talked to you?" Romy asked before he took a bite of cheese.

"My sisters are consumed with curiosity about you."

"Your sisters?"

"I told you I have five, right? Well, they all work together, except one who's made motherhood her career." Kit paused. "*We* all work together."

"A family business. That's nice."

"Yeah, I guess. It's not what I want to do with the rest of my life."

"What do you want to do?"

"I don't know, but something else."

Romy smiled. Sometimes Kit sounded like an eighth grader on a long car trip, but it didn't bother Romy. In fact, he found it endearing. "I'm sure it'll come to you," he said. "Are your sisters younger, older?"

"I'm the youngest."

"Wow, five *older* sisters. I have no words. I just have the one brother."

"I always wanted a brother. Or two. Or three!" Kit laughed.

"I always wanted a little sister."

"I *need* an older brother to take the pressure off."

"It's not easy being the only son, I guess."

"Well, you know, my mom and dad expect me to carry on the family name."

"They don't know you're gay?"

Kit shook his head. "More wine?" he said as he held up the bottle.

"Sure." Romy held out his glass. "My brother knows I'm gay, and he's okay with it. My mom pretends she doesn't, but I know she does. We just don't ever talk about it."

"I'd settle for that."

"I feel bad that she gets left out of that part of my life. When I fall in love, I want to be able to introduce you to her."

"You?"

"Me what?"

"You said 'introduce *you* to her.' I think you meant to say *him*."

"Freudian slip, I guess."

Kit smiled at his wine. "I'm kind of superstitious," he said. "And I don't want to jinx things, but I have to say again how much I like being with you."

"Me too. Do you do that thing where you keep wondering when something's going to go wrong? It kind of spooks me that the more I know you, the more I like you."

"Me too."

Silence fell as Romy leaned slowly toward Kit and Kit met him halfway. Their lips met, parted, and met again, one kiss leading into another. Romy set down his glass and cupped Kit's cheek in his palm. His fingertips slipped into the silky hair at Kit's temple as his mouth moved gently on Kit's. Kit put his free hand on Romy's shoulder, fingers gripping hard muscle as he returned the kiss, subtly increasing the pressure of his lips on Romy's.

"Wow," Romy said as he drew back. "We should save making out for later, or we might as well forget about the dinner and the movie and go straight to the sex."

"I wouldn't complain."

"Hey, I'm as turned on as you are, but—"

"I doubt it," Kit interrupted.

"You'll have to take my word for it right now. After dinner and the movie, I'll show you."

"Why do we have to wait?"

"Because as tempting as you are—and you are the definition of tempting—some things shouldn't be rushed. They deserve to happen in their own time. I have too much respect for the thing I hope is happening between us to—"

"Okay, I understand," Kit interrupted again. "I'm going to check on the stew."

Romy was thrown, but only for a moment. "I'll come with you," he said as he rose.

Kit took the lid off the big pot and a wonderful aroma filled the kitchen. He stirred the contents a few times, tasted the stew, and put the lid back on. "It's hot enough," he said. "Would you open that bottle while I get some bowls and spoons?"

"I'm not sure I need more alcohol," Romy said.

"Hey, don't fuck with my plan," Kit replied as he ladled stew into a big bowl.

Romy busied himself with the corkscrew while Kit put the bowls, spoons, and an assortment of small side dishes on a tray. With Romy carrying the bottle and fresh glasses, they went back to the living room. Kit set the tray on the coffee table and picked up a remote control that looked like it belonged on a starship.

"What are we watching?" Romy asked as Kit pressed a button.

"*Were the World Mine.* Have you seen it?"

Romy shook his head. "What's it about?"

"It's impossible to explain in a few words, but it's a great movie."

A sudden blast of noise from the speakers made Romy jump.

"Sorry," Kit said. "I was listening to music earlier. Okay, here's the movie."

For the next one hundred minutes, Romy and Kit sat and watched a movie about a bullied young gay man who invents a love potion. The film encompassed slapstick comedy, high school angst, Shakespeare, random bursts of whimsy, and full-on musical numbers. Romy was charmed and Kit was gratified that his favorite movie was appreciated.

"No, really, I loved it," Romy said for about the fortieth time. "It was as good as your stew. Please relax. I'm having a great time." He paused as he took a long look at Kit. "It surprises me that you're this insecure."

"I'm only human."

"Only a human with a gorgeous face and body, hot car, and killer apartment. I imagine everyone in your life loves you and you've got guys falling at your feet. I'm still amazed I'm the one here with you, instead of some stud in an Armani suit."

"I thought we agreed we were just two people."

"Yeah, I seem to remember that. All right, I'll try not to throw your money in your face again."

"Thank you. Did you really like the stew?"

"I ate three bowls of it."

"Some people think it's too spicy."

"I think it's just right."

Kit smiled as he hugged a throw pillow to his chest. "I'm so happy right now," he said.

"I'd really like to kiss you right now."

Kit tossed the pillow over his shoulder and leaned toward Romy. Romy closed the rest of the distance and kissed Kit's forehead. With a soft laugh, Kit tilted his head until his lips found Romy's. He moved closer and the corner of the couch cushion crumpled, tumbling him into Romy's lap. Both men cracked up, as Romy collapsed onto his back with Kit on top of him. Kit looked down into Romy's eyes as his merriment morphed into unabashed desire.

Romy reached up to stroke Kit's hair back from his face and let his hand drift down as Kit leaned in to kiss him. As he and Kit exchanged a series of increasingly bolder kisses, Romy explored Kit's anatomy. Stroking, squeezing, and kneading, he made his way down Kit's back to his butt and up to his neck again. Framing Kit's face between his hands, Romy took control of the kiss, sliding his tongue between Kit's lips.

Kit returned the kiss eagerly, his tongue flirting with Romy's as he ran his fingers down Romy's sides to the hem of his shirt. Working his hands under the soft fabric, he slid his fingers over the firm contours of Romy's abs and chest. He found Romy's nipples already taut, and he smiled into the kiss, happy with the effect he was having. Breaking the kiss, he dipped his head to take a nipple between his teeth in a tender bite.

When Romy started to sit up, Kit urged him to stay down while sucking at his nipple through the T-shirt. Romy moaned at the exquisite friction of the wet fabric against his sensitive skin as Kit tongued the tip. He arched into the caress, losing himself in the rush of intense pleasure.

The doorbell rang and Kit's head shot up. "Who the hell?" he muttered as the chimes sounded again. He looked down into Romy's eyes. "If we're quiet, maybe they'll go away," Kit said.

Romy rose on his elbows to kiss Kit. "Answer your door," he said.

"Why?"

"Because fate can't be avoided, only diverted."

"What?"

"Clearly, it isn't the right moment for us to do this." Romy paused as the doorbell rang again. He gave Kit another quick kiss and pushed him gently away. "Go." He looked down at the wet spot on his shirt. "Where'd you put my sweatshirt?" he asked.

Kit tossed the sweatshirt to Romy on his way to the door. He took a glance at the entryway mirror and ran a hand through his hair. The doorbell rang again as he reached for the knob. "You are going to be so sorry," he said under his breath to the persistent bell ringer.

"Kissy!" A tall young man brushed past Kit into the apartment. "I brought booze." He brandished a bottle. "Let's drink!"

Kit put a hand against the wall to trap his friend in the hallway. "Not tonight, Ash," he said. "I have a guest."

"The more the merrier." The tall man tried to see around Kit. "Who is it?" He raised his voice. "Who's in there?"

"None of your business. Be a friend and just go away, please?" Kit herded Ash back to the open door.

"Why don't you want me to meet your friend?"

Kit glared at the other man. "We're busy," he said in a fierce whisper.

"Oh." Ash snickered. "I'm sorry. But it's your fault. You should tip the doorman to keep people away when you're getting some action. I'll go and let you get back to—"

"Don't worry about it," Romy said from behind Kit. "I need to get home anyway."

"Hi, I'm Horace Ashford," Ash said quickly, trying to step into Romy's path. "I prefer to be called Ash for obvious reasons. And you are?"

"Leave him alone," Kit hissed at Ash. "Romy, wait!"

"I have to be up early. I'll call you." Romy smiled over his shoulder as he left.

"Thank you. Thank you very much," Kit told Ash.

CHAPTER
NINE

"GIVE ME a break," Ash said as Kit turned away from him. "How was I to know you were in seduction mode?"

"Why are you so dense? You should've just left. Now Romy thinks I'm embarrassed to be seen with him."

"That guy? The one that just left?" Ash shook his head as he followed Kit. "Honey, he's got nothing to be embarrassed about. What did he have stuffed down the front of his pants anyway? It looked like missile-launch time down there."

"Thanks to you, the mission was scrubbed."

"I'm truly sorry, Kissy. Truly."

Kit sighed. "Let's see the bottle," he said.

Ash handed over the expensive tequila. "Your brand, I believe," he said.

"You're not forgiven, but come on in."

"I don't blame you," Ash said as he followed Kit. "He's hot. Hey, he's not straight, is he?"

"I'm really tired of that question," Kit said as he went into the kitchen.

"He didn't trip my gaydar, is the only reason I ask."

Kit put two shot glasses on the counter. "Gaydar is bullshit."

"I'd ask why you're so pissy if I didn't already know." Ash came over to lean against Kit's back. "I'm sorry I cockblocked you." He slid his hands around Kit's waist to cup his crotch. "Let me make it up to you."

Kit shook Ash off. "No thanks."

"You're turning down one of *my* blow jobs?" Ash affected a voice choked with emotion. "I just don't know you anymore, man."

"I've changed that much since last weekend?"

"We usually get together for drinks after work. I haven't seen you all week. You don't answer my calls, and when I text you, you just say you're busy. Now that I've seen Romy, I understand, but you could've at least given me a clue."

"I'm not ready to talk about it. It's too soon."

"You don't want to jinx it," Ash guessed. "I get it, and you know I'd never stand in the way of you getting some."

"Thanks."

"So… how's the oingo-boingo? Is he as good as he looks?"

"We haven't slept together yet."

"Who cares. I want to know if you've fucked him yet."

"No."

"Oh. That's a shame. So… is he an actor? A model?"

"A mechanic. He fixed my car."

"No shit? Next time my car needs servicing I'm taking it in myself."

"I don't think you'll find another Romy. He's really… special."

"You don't say." Ash pretended to study Kit. "Christopher Davis Britten, are you in love?" He drew out the last word in a lilting drawl.

"Would it be such a shock?"

"Yes." Ash picked up the bottle and poured two shots. "Not only did you have one of the most spectacularly painful breakups I've ever witnessed, you actually swore you wouldn't fall in love again. Vowed it."

"I was a kid when I said that."

"It was two years ago." Ash took a drink. "I'm not trying to depress you. I'm trying to act like a friend. I'd hate to see you hurt like that again."

"That could never happen. *He's* married now and lives in Tokyo, of all places."

"That's not what I meant, and you know it. Is there any reason I shouldn't meet this Romy and interrogate him?"

"You'll scare him off."

"So it's not okay for me to abduct him, tie him naked to a bed, and—"

"No!" Kit said loudly. "It's not okay. Don't question him. Don't even talk to him. Stay away from him."

"Calm down, Kissy. I'm just kidding."

"Try to be funny next time." Kit poured two more shots and they drank. "Seriously, though, don't go near Romy. And stop calling me Kissy."

"I promise. Pinky swear."

"He's a really decent guy, and he doesn't need to know my past just yet."

"I understand." Ash pursed his lips. "Sort of." He squinted his eyes. "No, not really. I don't understand what's wrong with your past."

"I don't want Romy to think my bed has a revolving door."

"Did you have it taken out?"

"Okay, so I've had a lot of boyfriends," Kit admitted.

"I know. I've been here since the show started at puberty."

"That was funny," Kit said. "And you're an asshole."

"Sorry, but I really have been right here for all the drama. I'm not criticizing you. You've always been such a hottie, and I see nothing wrong in using what nature gave you. Plus, sex is fun. It's just that you always manage to pick the wrong guy. Things seem fine at first, but it always turns out that they're not ready for your idea of what being in love is." Ash shrugged. "Their loss."

"I always try to change them. I'm so stupid."

"You're not stupid. You're just… hopeful."

"But you're right. I always pick the wrong guy."

"I may have exaggerated. There wasn't anything all that wrong with them. They just weren't ready."

"For what? Ash, if you know what's wrong with me, you have to tell me."

"There's nothing wrong with you. But the men you've fallen for weren't ready or strong enough to handle your love. You're like a tsunami, my friend, a no-shit force of nature, and when you turn your full attention on someone, it can be a little overwhelming."

"I've tried dialing it back."

"That makes me sad." Ash put a hand on the back of Kit's neck and touched their foreheads together. "You should just be yourself, all of yourself, and not just bits and pieces of you. If Romy's the right man, he'll be able to deal with it. And you won't have any reason to worry about awkward secrets."

"Because honesty works so well for you?" Kit asked as he drew back.

"That sounds like you're calling me out. Okay, I accept your challenge. If you'll tell everyone you're gay, I will too. I'll break off my engagement and tell the truth about why I'm doing it."

"Forget it. This isn't a subject for a drunken bet."

"No blow jobs. No drunk bets. You really have changed."

Kit chuckled. "This is why you've been my best friend forever. You can see humor in almost anything."

Ash smiled. "Remember high school? When you, me, Teddy, and Park were the Fabulous Four?"

"No, I've completely forgotten about it."

Ash laughed. "Everyone wanted us or wanted to be us."

"Yeah, but that was high school."

"I know. I'm trying to say that I'm glad you aren't stuck in high school like some of the other people we know."

"What are you talking about? I live in an apartment owned by my dad's corporation. I do odd jobs for my sister. I drive a car I got for my birthday. Does that sound like a grown-up to you?"

"I didn't say you were a grown-up. I'd never insult you like that. I think you'd make an excellent rebel, though."

"And what exactly would I be rebelling against?"

"The usual. Injustice. Intolerance. Inequality. All the big ones." Ash cleared his throat. "Not to mention your parents."

"Why does everyone want me to come out?"

"I can only speak for my own motives. I actually *want* to come out, but I'm afraid to do it alone." Ash sighed. "We're not getting younger. Eventually, it'll become obvious what we are. If we reveal it ourselves, at least we can control how it happens."

"That's what my sister said, more or less. I just don't know if I'm ready to live as an openly gay person. You know how much my family means to me. If they disowned me, I'd be destroyed."

"Your sisters already know you're gay, and they still love you."

"They're not my parents."

"I don't want to argue about it. I'm just throwing it out there."

"Coming out isn't like deciding to jump in the car and drive to the beach to see the sun come up."

"I know that. Pour me another shot. This deep and meaningful conversation has killed my buzz for reals."

"New subject. Who were you drinking with before you came here?"

"A pack of your exes."

"Ha ha."

"No really. Behr was there. Um, who else? Lee Campbell, Teddy Fonteyn, and Parker Ellis. And me, of course."

"Very funny."

"Come on. It's not *that* farfetched."

"That doesn't make it better."

"I can't please you tonight. I guess I'll go find someone more receptive to my sparkling repartee."

"I won't beg you to stay. And next time, call before you come over."

"Noted." Ash went to the door. "When do you want to get together again?"

"You're coming to Eliza's annual barbecue weekend after next, right? I'm thinking about asking Romy. You two could meet officially."

"I wouldn't miss it. Good night, Kissy."

Kit shut the door and leaned back on it as he turned his gaze up to the ceiling. "My life is going so well," he observed. "I've never been happier. What does that mean?"

He cleaned up the kitchen, put away the leftover food, and got ready for bed. After answering a few emails, he put his laptop aside and turned on the bedroom television. He dimmed the lights, snuggled down in the bed, and feel asleep watching *Were the World Mine* again.

In the morning, Kit got out of bed immediately instead of lazing around for a while chasing the tail of a dream. He dressed quickly and left his apartment by seven. Picking up coffee from a drive-through, he went straight to Romy's garage. Monday-morning traffic was indifferent to his need for speed and it took almost an hour to reach his destination.

Kit pulled into the gravel parking lot and waited for a customer to leave before he got out of his car. As he waited, he could feel Romy's gaze each time Romy glanced out the window, and he was slightly on edge as he walked into the office.

"This is a nice surprise," Romy said.

"Is it?"

"Of course it is." Romy pursed his lips. "Why wouldn't it be?"

"You left in such a hurry last night," Kit said.

"I thought I explained that I had to be up early."

"I just want to be sure it wasn't something I did. If I went too far with the necking...." Kit let his voice trail off.

"I can see you're genuinely concerned, and it's in poor taste for me to be amused by it, but damn it, I am kind of tickled at you apologizing like some Victorian gentleman who bruised the tender sensibilities of a blushing virgin."

"Do I really sound like that?"

"A little bit. Enough to make me smile."

"So... we're okay?"

"We're fine. It was a little awkward when your friend dropped by, but—"

"I'm not ashamed of you," Kit said quickly. "It's my friends. I'm afraid they aren't good enough for you."

"Why would you say that?"

"I only have one real friend, the one you saw last night. Our moms met in college and became best friends, so we've known each other all our lives. He's a good guy."

"But?" Romy smiled. "I hear a *but* in there somewhere."

"I'm afraid you'll think I'm shallow."

"I won't."

"You might when you find out how I spend most of my time."

"Lately, you've been spending a lot of your time with me."

"Because that's all I've wanted to do since I met you." Kit bit his lip. "If you find out about my past, you might not want to spend time with me."

"Have you ever been cruel to an animal?"

"Of course not."

"Ever hurt anyone on purpose?"

Kit shook his head.

"Do you think it's just wrong that spiders can be considered pets?"

Kit shuddered.

"So how bad could it be?"

"I spend most of my free time in bars or someone's bed, while pretending to my family that I'm a good boy looking for the right girl."

"That sounds pretty normal."

"But I'm not normal, am I? I like men."

"I, for one, am very thankful."

Kit paused before he spoke again. "Why do you like me so much?" he asked.

"I've thought about that actually. I liked you as soon as I saw you standing in the oil stains in your fuzzy pink sweater. The best way I can say it is that you're just so *you*."

"Maybe I am when I'm with you, but when I'm with my parents, I'm a big phony."

"If it bothers you so much, then stop lying to them."

"You make it sound simple."

"Simple to do, tough to live with."

Kit gave Romy an inquiring look.

"You may have noticed that I'm not exactly overflowing with business. That's because no one wants their car fixed by the queer. I came out to my friends a while back. Some of them were cool with it, like Joplin, but some of them weren't. The ones that weren't went around telling everyone in the neighborhood there was a homo in their midst."

"Couldn't you move?"

"I will as soon as I save up enough money."

"Can't you get a loan?"

"You're kidding, right? Who's going to lend me money?"

"I would."

"Thanks, but I'll be fine. It'll just take a little while."

Kit changed the subject. "Are you busy tonight?"

"I'm having dinner with my family. It's a Monday-night thing."

"Oh. Okay. How about tomorrow?"

"Sure, but you can come to Mom's with me tonight if you want."

"Really?"

"Yeah, really. Be here at six thirty, and you can drive. Cardo will explode when he sees your car."

"I'll be here by six thirty."

"Good. Just one more thing."

"What?"

"Why did your friend Ash call you Kissy?"

"Oh, God." Kit made a strangled noise. "My sisters called me that when I was a baby and it stuck."

"It's kind of cute."

"No," Kit said. "Don't you dare."

"Okay." Romy shrugged. "Now go to work and let me go do mine."

Kit leaned over the counter and gave Romy a quick kiss. "See you later," he said as he walked away.

Romy looked around, but he didn't think anyone had seen the kiss. "I must be out of my mind," he said as he watched Kit pull out of the parking lot in his shiny, bright-red car. "He's way out of my league."

CHAPTER

TEN

"REALLY?" ROMY said when Kit showed up at the garage the next evening. "You wore a suit?"

"I'm meeting your mother for the first time. I want to make a good impression." Kit smoothed the front of his navy sports jacket. "And it's not a suit. It's a jacket and trousers."

"That *is* a tie, though, right?"

"Is it really too much?"

"I'm just teasing you. However… the giant bouquet and gift basket might be a bit over the top."

"They can stay in the car."

"Relax, babe. Remember to just be yourself."

Kit took a deep breath. "Okay. Why don't you drive?"

As predicted, Romy's fourteen-year-old brother went crazy over Kit's car. After Kit went with Cardo on an illegal drive around the block with the fourteen-year-old at the wheel, Cardo was ready to welcome him into the family. Mrs. O'Keefe was charmed by the tie, the basket of gourmet food, and the lavish flowers.

"I'm so happy my Romy is making nice friends," Mrs. O'Keefe said as she set yet another plate in front of Kit. "I can see that you're a nice boy."

"I try to be," Kit said. "Can I talk you into telling me the spices you put in your crab stew?"

Cardo drew Romy aside as Kit and Mrs. O'Keefe compared recipes. "So?" he said.

"So what?"

"Is this *the* guy?"

"What do you mean?"

"Come on, big brother. Not once have you ever brought a guy to the house. I figure this one must be special." Cardo glanced toward the dining room. "He's got good manners."

"I'm glad you approve."

"I just wanted you to know that it's cool."

"Good." Romy suppressed a smile. "Is that all you wanted to say?"

"Don't be an asshat."

"Okay, I'm seriously glad you approve."

"Mom does too. I can tell."

"Don't be ridiculous."

"She told me she'd rather see you happy with a man than go through life alone."

"Mom said that?"

Cardo nodded. "I guess it's up to me to give her grandchildren."

"You don't need to get started on that just yet."

"Relax. I've got plans. First college and then marriage."

"Good luck with that."

"That sounded sarcastic."

"I'm just saying that plans don't always work out. Some cute freshman might wink at you, and the next thing you know, you're changing diapers and working nights to pay the rent."

Cardo shook his head. "Not this guy. You know mom would kick my ass if I got a girl pregnant."

"And you know I'd be in line right behind her."

"Tough guy." Cardo pulled Romy into a hug.

"Sorry you had to have a fag for a big brother."

"I don't like that word," Cardo said. "I've beat guys up for calling you that."

"You have?"

"It's only fair. You protected me from bullies when I was little."

"Romy! Cardo? Where are you, boys?" Mrs. O'Keefe called out.

"Coming, Mom," Cardo said. "Just needed some big-brotherly advice."

"Stop talking about girls and get in here. It's time for dessert."

Cardo smirked at Romy. "Yeah, stop talking about girls," he whispered.

Romy smacked the back of Cardo's head and dashed back into the dining room. Cardo followed Romy at a slower pace. Mrs. O'Keefe gave each of her sons an inquiring look but neither responded.

"Always up to something," Mrs. O'Keefe said. "You should have seen Romy when he was Cardo's age, Kit. No one could keep up with him."

"I wish I *had* known Romy in school," Kit said. "I think we would've been friends."

"Well, you're friends now." Mrs. O'Keefe smiled and stood up. "I'll be right back with dessert."

"Your mom is so cool," Kit said after Mrs. O'Keefe went into the kitchen.

"We like her," Romy said.

"And she likes you," Cardo told Kit. "I like you too." He glanced at Romy. "I hope my brother has the good sense to hold on to you."

Romy jabbed his elbow into Cardo's ribs.

"Ow!" Cardo yelped as Mrs. O'Keefe came back into the room.

"Are you all right?" she asked, as she set the strawberry cream cake on the table.

"I'm fine," Cardo said. "Just got a splinter in my butt."

Mrs. O'Keefe didn't look like she believed him, but she let it drop and began slicing the cake. She gave everyone a large wedge and a fork and watched them eat. Without thinking, Kit wiped a smear of icing off Romy's chin and put his finger in his mouth.

"Excuse my bad manners," he said when he realized everyone was looking at him.

"Don't give it a thought," Mrs. O'Keefe said. "I've seen a lot worse over the years."

Cardo laughed. "Remember the time the neighbors asked if we had a cat and Romy told them the litter box was for him?"

"How could I forget?" Mrs. O'Keefe shook her head, but she smiled fondly at Romy.

The family started telling Romy-stories and Kit was sorry when Romy said it was time to go. As Mrs. O'Keefe walked with them to the door, she told Kit he was welcome to come back anytime he liked. Kit waited in the hall, while Romy turned back and kissed his mother on the cheek, as he slipped an envelope into her hand. Kit pretended not to see the exchange or the tears of gratitude in Mrs. O'Keefe's eyes.

"So," Kit said, as he pulled the car out of the parking space. "You're supporting your family?"

"I help when I can. Mom has a job, but Cardo's still in school, so it's tough to make ends meet."

"Don't be defensive. I think it's great what you're doing."

"Call me old-fashioned, but I'm the oldest son, so...."

"So you take responsibility." Kit nodded. "You know, if we were allowed to get married, your family would be my family, and I could help support them."

"That's really sweet. Are you thinking of proposing to me?"

"With every beat of my heart." Kit looked over at Romy. "Don't laugh."

"Sorry. I'm counting myself lucky that you're paying attention to me, and you're booking a honeymoon cruise."

"Okay, go ahead and make fun. I love your sense of humor."

"I love that you love my sense of humor."

"What kind of cruise?"

"What?"

"What kind of cruise would you like to go on?"

"I've always wanted to go to Cozumel. All the pictures look so... perfect. You know?"

"It's really nice there once you get away from the touristy areas."

"There's just something about water that particular shade of blue."

"I agree. We should go."

"I'd love to do that someday. It's a really nice dream to look forward to."

"I just want to see you in a Speedo."

"Lunatic."

"Hey! Only my friends can call me lunatic."

"Can I call you lunatic?"

"Of course. You're my friend, aren't you?"

"Yes, I am. Cardo said Mom really likes you."

"I really like her. And Cardo."

"Even though he'd sell you into the sex trade for this car?"

"Even though." Kit grinned. "Your family is really cool."

"You missed the turn," Romy said.

"It's not even ten yet. I thought you might want to have a drink somewhere."

"I can't tonight. Someone's dropping a car off at five tomorrow morning."

"Just stay up all night."

"I've done that too many times. I know the value of sleep now. Make a left here and another left in two blocks."

Kit sighed. "Fine." He drove around the block and pulled in at the garage. As he put the car in park, he turned to kiss Romy.

Romy put a hand under Kit's chin and leaned into the kiss. He kept hold of Kit's jaw as he broke the kiss and drew back to look into Kit's eyes. "I want you more than I've ever wanted anything," he said. "But I really need to get some sleep."

"Can we just make out in the car for a while?"

Romy stroked his fingertips down Kit's neck to his collar. "We could, but I'd probably lose track of time."

"I'll walk you to your door."

"No, we'll say good night right here, and then I'll get out of your tasty car and walk away. You'll drive home and get a good night's sleep."

"You're going to kiss me good night, aren't you?"

"I thought I did."

"Think again." Kit tangled his fist in Romy's hair and pulled Romy into a torrid kiss. Using lips, tongue, and teeth, Kit devoured Romy's mouth in a frank declaration of desire. He sucked gently at Romy's tongue before letting it go in favor of Romy's ripe bottom lip. Several nibbles later, Kit slowly ended the kiss and let Romy go. "Now you've been kissed good night," he said.

"Thoroughly," Romy agreed. He touched his lips gently to Kit's and got out of the car. "I'll call you tomorrow," he said.

"No," Kit said. "I'll call *you* tomorrow."

"Lunatic." Romy smiled as he turned and walked around the side of the garage.

"Wait!" Kit called out.

Romy stepped back out into the light. "What?"

"Want to go to my sister's barbecue with me on Saturday? She has this big bash every year for family and friends. You can hide in the crowd if you want."

"You want me there?"

"I'm asking, aren't I?"

"Okay. Now leave. We can talk about this later."

Kit blew Romy a kiss and drove away.

"Sweet, sweet lunatic," Romy said, watching until Kit was out of sight before going inside.

CHAPTER
ELEVEN

ROMY GLANCED at the clock and then at his phone as he'd been doing every five minutes. It was after noon and Kit hadn't called. Romy had called Kit's cell three times, and each time he'd been sent to voice mail. He was still composing a message in his head that he intended to record the next time he called. Five more minutes went by and Romy picked up the phone. He was surprised when someone answered.

"Hello. This is Kit Britten's phone."

"Who is this?" Romy asked.

"Horace Ashford. Who is this?"

"Jerome O'Keefe."

"Romy! I'm glad you called."

"Why didn't Kit answer?"

"Because I have his phone." Ash paused. "Oh. Right, you don't know what happened. Well, Kit got into some trouble last night. He's fine, don't worry, but he's on some very effective pain meds at the moment. I'm not sure he knows where he is."

"What happened?"

"A couple of guys tried to carjack the Ferrari. Kit wasn't inclined to let them have it. They knocked him around some, but the cops showed up before any real damage was done. The painkillers are for his jaw. It's pretty bruised up but not dislocated or anything."

"When are visiting hours over?"

"Don't bother, honey. Kit's being discharged in a couple of hours. I'll tell him to call you as soon as he can talk. I'm sure it's the first thing he'll want to do when he's coherent."

"Is he really okay?"

"Yeah, he really is. He's got some nasty bruises, but no broken bones or anything."

Romy breathed a deep sigh of relief. "Thanks," he said.

"I'll tell him you asked about him. I know that'll make him feel better."

"Thanks again."

"No problem. Hey, I'll see you at the barbecue, right?"

"Sure. Bye." Romy hung up and set the phone down. His fingers were shaking and he could barely swallow past the lump in his throat. Kit had been attacked, and he hadn't known about it for hours. What if the carjackers had carried guns? Romy was struck by the cold reality that he could lose Kit so easily, and in the same moment, he realized how much Kit had come to mean to him in such a short time. He brooded about it until his phone rang as he was closing up shop. He didn't recognize the number.

"Hello, this is Romy O'Keefe," he said.

"You don't sound very sure of that."

"Kit!" Romy exclaimed. "I was so worried about you. Where are you?"

"I'm at my parents' house."

"Your parents?" Romy echoed.

"Yes." Kit said, obviously talking to someone besides Romy. "Even though there's nothing wrong with me and I'm perfectly capable of taking care of myself, I'm being forced to stay with my parents."

"Is someone in the room with you?" Romy asked.

"My sisters are watching me like hawks. Like teams of hawks."

Romy chuckled. "I'm sure you're going crazy, but I'm glad you're being looked after."

"I don't need looking after." Kit raised his voice again. "No, I *don't*. If you repeat that crap about concussions one more time, I'll throw this ice cream at you. Now go away and let me talk in privacy, please." He lowered his voice again. "Sorry, Romy. They're treating me like I broke all my arms and legs."

"You don't want to mess around with a concussion," Romy said.

Kit made a disgusted sound. "Not you too!"

"Just eat your ice cream and take it easy. When can I see you?"

"I don't know," Kit said. "Depends on when the warden lets me out."

"Maybe I could push you around the park in a wheelchair."

"I can feel you smirking."

"You sound all right. Are you? Really?"

"Yes. I got punched and kicked, and I'm sore and bruised, and I'll probably mumble for a while, but I'm fine. Their goal wasn't to hurt me. They just wanted the car."

"I wish I'd been with you when it happened."

"I like that tone in your voice," Kit purred.

Romy cleared his throat. "Well, I guess it's a good thing the cops showed up."

"My car has a gizmo that alerts the police when you push the button or say the code word."

"Cool. The car wasn't damaged, was it? Cardo will want to know."

Kit chuckled. "The car is fine. Not a scratch on it."

"Good." Romy paused. "I wish I could see you right now."

"So do I." Kit sighed.

"I could come over after work."

"I want to see you, but it would be so awkward here. I wouldn't be able to kiss you or touch you the way I want to. I'm afraid I might have an aneurysm if I could see you but couldn't hold you."

"I actually understand that." Romy leaned back against a workbench. "Right now, I want to hold you so much. I want to hug you and kiss you and make sure you're really all right."

"You're perfect. Did you know that? The perfect boyfriend."

"Am I your boyfriend?"

"I hope so. Don't you want to be my boyfriend?"

"Of course, but I didn't want to be pushy, you know?"

"It's one of my favorite things about you. You respect other people."

"Why wouldn't I?"

"Oh, you know, a lot people have this attitude like 'you have to *earn* my respect.'"

"I tend to give people respect until they show me they don't deserve it."

"I've noticed." Kit relaxed against the bank of pillows propped behind him. "You're just such a... *man*. I mean... well, you're honest and you work hard. You honor your mother and help support your family. You don't take things for granted." Kit slowed down. "I'm probably saying this all wrong, but I think you're wonderful. Hey! I'm still talking! Get out!"

"Kit?"

"Get out!"

"Kit?"

"Sorry. One of my sisters thinks it's imperative that my temperature gets checked right this second. Get away with that thing! I'm talking to someone! Sorry, Romy, I'm going to have to go now. They're relentless."

"Let them take care of you."

"I will. Honestly, I think they love it when I'm a brat."

"You *are* awfully cute when you act spoiled."

"Damn. I really have to hang up now. Mom's here."

"Please take care of yourself."

"I'll call you as soon as I can."

"I'll be waiting," Romy said, but Kit was gone.

After locking the garage, Romy didn't feel like being alone, so he walked to his Mom's apartment. He told them what he knew about the attempted carjacking and let his mother comfort him with hugs while his little brother swore vengeance on the thugs who'd dared lay hands on Kit and the Ferrari. When he left for home, he felt much better. When his phone rang and he saw Kit's number, his spirits rose immeasurably.

"Hi, how are you?" he said as he answered.

"Mom made me take more painkillers. I'm fine, but I doubt I could make it to the bathroom by myself. My legs have turned into boiled noodles."

"At least you'll get a good night's sleep."

"I've been sleeping on and off *all day*. I hate just lying here."

"Turn on the TV."

"It makes me sleepy."

"I'm sensing a theme here. Maybe you should just stop fighting it and go to sleep."

"I hate this."

Romy pictured Kit in a bed as fluffy and white as a cloud, with his cheeks flushed and his sweet lips drooping in a pout. "I wish I was there to give you a hug, but since I'm not, how would you like me to sing you a song?"

The petulant tone disappeared from Kit's voice. "Am I being that big a baby?"

"Yes. That's why I'm offering to sing a lullaby. Do you want it or not?"

"Yes, please."

"Are you lying down?"

"Yeah." Kit snuggled into his pillows.

"What are you wearing?"

Kit laughed softly and a wave of warmth swept through Romy. "Are you ready?" he murmured.

"I'm ready."

Softly, Romy sang into the phone as he walked:

"Go to sleep, precious child.

I know the winter night is wild.

But I promise I will be right here.

There's nothing that you have to fear.

You're safe with me so close your eyes,

while thunder crashes in the skies.

Go to sleep, little one, though the rain has drowned the sun.

I promise I will be right here.

There's nothing that you need to fear.

You're safe with me so close your eyes,

while thunder crashes in the skies."

"That was beautiful," Kit said drowsily.

"Good night." Romy put away his phone and walked the rest of the way home, lost in sweet thoughts of a sleeping Kit. These thoughts accompanied him to bed, and he dreamed the night away until the phone woke him.

TWELVE

ROMY GRABBED the phone off the night table. "Romy O'Keefe," he said.

"What are you doing?"

"Good morning, Kit."

"Answer the question."

"I'm getting out of bed."

"Can you skip work today? Or leave early? I'm finally being allowed to go home and I'd love to see you as soon as possible."

"Let me make some arrangements, and I'll call you back, okay?"

"Okay. Call me soon."

"I will. Bye." Romy put down the phone and got out of bed. He stretched and looked down at his hard-on. "That last dream was a good one, wasn't it?" he said to his crotch.

Romy turned on the water in his small shower and stepped in. He washed his hair and then reached for the soap. The warm spray played over his body, rinsing off the lather and conjuring images of Kit, wet and naked. Romy put down the soap and took hold of his cock, stroking it slowly at first, but increasing the pace as his climax built. As he crested, Romy could almost hear Kit panting his name. Romy leaned against the fiberglass wall of the shower, sinking his teeth into his lower lip as he spurted and his come joined the falling water.

"Wow," he breathed as he turned off the shower and reached for a towel.

He knew he was going to get dressed and go to Kit. He was going to close the garage for the day, even though he might lose some business. His need to see Kit was greater than his need to make money. When did that happen? *Oh, yeah, right. That happened when I found out that Kit had been in danger.*

Romy turned from that line of thought and got dressed. Honestly, he didn't have any urgent work, so he locked up the garage, put out the *Closed* sign, and walked a few blocks to the bus stop. As he walked, he called Kit.

"Are you on your way?" Kit said as he answered.

"I'm getting on the first bus right now."

"We have to get you a car. I can see it's going to be a necessity."

"Yeah, we really should do that." Romy laughed. "Lunatic."

"Just get here as fast as you can."

"That's what I'm doing."

"Good."

"I'll see you soon."

The words *I love you* sprang to Kit's lips, but he brushed them away. It was way too soon to blurt out things like that, no matter how open he was being. "Okay. Bye," he said.

In slightly more than half an hour, Romy rang Kit's doorbell. As he waited in the hall, he pulled down the hem of his white T-shirt and shifted the denim jacket on his shoulders.

"Come on in," Kit said when he answered the door. "My sister Jules is here," he added quickly.

Romy followed Kit into the living room. Before they sat down, a young woman entered from the kitchen.

"Romy O'Keefe, this is my sister Jules," Kit said.

"It's a pleasure to meet you," Romy said.

"The pleasure is mine," Jules said.

"Stop flirting," Kit told his sister.

"I was being courteous. Are you really that jealous?"

"Yes. Can you make some coffee?"

"Just give me a few minutes." Jules disappeared back into the kitchen.

"She won't leave," Kit whispered.

Romy leaned in and kissed Kit before drawing back and casting a glance at the kitchen door. "I'm so glad you're all right," he said.

"It was scary, but I'm all right. Thank you for singing me to sleep last night."

Romy ducked his head, smiling shyly.

"I love your voice," Kit went on. "Maybe you'll sing for me again."

Romy gently touched a fingertip to the storm-cloud-colored bruise that darkened the fair skin along Kit's jaw line. "Does it hurt a lot?"

"Not with the drugs I'm taking. Look at this." Kit peeled up his pink T-shirt and Romy gasped at the bruises on Kit's ribs. "They look a lot worse than they are," Kit said.

"I'm sorry I wasn't there."

"Don't feel that way. It wasn't your responsibility to take care of me."

"I want to take of care of you. I—" Romy broke off as Jules returned.

"I know how Kissy likes his coffee," she said. "How would you like yours, Romy?"

"Didn't I tell you to stop flirting?" Kit said.

Romy smiled. "Black is fine," he told Jules.

Jules smiled at Romy, glared at her brother, and went back to the kitchen.

"What were you saying?" Kit asked.

Romy cleared his throat. "We need to have a serious talk, but I'd like to do it in private."

Kit's eyes got big. "You're making me nervous," he said.

Romy started to speak, but Jules came back with the coffee and sat down on the chair opposite the couch.

"I can see why Kit's been keeping you all to himself," Jules said before taking a demure sip of her coffee.

"Thank you," Romy said.

"I hope the family will be seeing more of you."

Kit finished his coffee in four large gulps. "I need fresh air," he announced.

Jules stared at her brother as he shot to his feet. "Do you need another pill?"

"No, I need to get out of here," Kit said. "I'm going for a walk."

"I'll get our jackets," Jules said.

"Romy can go with me," Kit said quickly. "Do you know where my sneakers are?"

Jules fetched Kit's shoes and he put them on. "Don't tire yourself," she said as Kit went to the door with Romy.

Kit took a windbreaker off a hook in the entryway. "If I pass out, Romy will carry me," he said. "Don't worry." He kissed the top of Jules's head. "Thanks for taking care of me."

"I'm your sister. Of course, I'm happy to care for you." Jules smiled. "I'm just going to clean up the kitchen and head home. I might be gone when you come back."

"Give my love to Riff and Raff."

"I will. The kittens miss you." Jules smiled at Romy. "It was good to meet you."

Kit hustled Romy out the door before he could answer. As soon as the elevator doors closed, Kit pressed Romy against the wall and pressed his full length against Romy as he took his mouth in an ardent kiss.

"I missed you so much," Kit said breathlessly as he let Romy come up for air. "I know it's only been a day, but it seems like forever since I kissed you good night."

Romy ran a hand through Kit's hair, cupping the back of his head as he pulled him into another kiss. "I just met you a couple of weeks ago, but now I couldn't stand it if something happened to take you away," he said.

The elevator doors opened and Kit and Romy walked across the lobby and out onto the sidewalk. Kit turned left and Romy kept pace with him until they reached Eleanor Tinsley Park.

"So what did you want to talk about?" Kit asked as they entered a shady path.

"I'm wondering if we should back off a little."

"I'm a little confused."

"And I'm a little scared of how much I care about you."

Kit was silent for several strides before he spoke. "Usually, guys are scared of how much I care for them. I seem to have found a new way to fuck things up."

"You didn't fuck anything up. I'm the one with the problem."

"Tell me why it scares you."

"For one thing, we live in different worlds. You were in the hospital and I didn't even know about it until hours later. I didn't like the way that made me feel. I don't want to be in love with you if we can't live our lives together. I couldn't live a half life only seeing you when we could both get away from our other lives. If we're going to be together, I want all of you."

Tears of relief shimmered in Kit's eyes. "I was afraid you were going to break up with me."

"I know it's too early to get serious, but I need to know you're at least willing to get serious."

"Yes." Kit took Romy's hand and drew him behind a screen of hedges. "I want this to be serious." He squeezed Romy's hand.

Romy put his arm around Kit's neck. "That's all I needed to know," he said in Kit's ear.

"You really had me worried," Kit said as he slipped his arms around Romy's waist.

"Sorry. I'm just a little gun shy."

"Did someone leave you?"

"Yeah, someone left me. Broke my heart." Romy gave Kit a squeeze. "But that was a long time ago, and I have you now."

"Yes, you do." Kit kissed Romy's cheek. "I have the strongest feeling I was meant to be with you."

"Hold on to that feeling and don't let anyone tell you it's nonsense." Romy let go of Kit when he heard voices on the other side of the hedge. The strollers moved on down the path and Romy shook his head at Kit. "I hate *that* feeling," he said.

"The feeling you're about to get caught doing something wrong?"

"That's the one," Romy said.

"I hate it too. We're not doing anything wrong, but everyone wants us to think we are."

"We'll have to see what we can do about that." Romy laced his fingers with Kit's and led him back to the path. "Meanwhile, it's almost time for lunch. Do you want to stop somewhere? Or I could make something for you at your place."

"I'm intrigued you can cook," Kit said. "I was afraid I'd have to do all the cooking after we got married."

"Lunatic," Romy said as he leaned in to brush his lips against Kit's hair.

Jules was gone when Kit and Romy got back to the apartment. While Kit read her note and followed the instructions, Romy went into the kitchen. By the time Kit had taken his meds, moved the laundry from the washer to the dryer, and changed his trousers for sweat pants, Romy had lunch ready.

"It's just an omelet," Romy said as Kit stared at his plate. "But I'm toasting some bread in the oven, and there's some—"

"Stop," Kit said. "It's the most beautiful, most perfect omelet in the history of eggs."

Romy handed Kit a fork. "I hope it tastes okay."

Kit took a bite. "Wow! This is amazing."

"I took a chance with the ingredients, but since they came out of your fridge, I figured you'd probably like them. Props for having cilantro, by the way."

"This is delicious. Can I just tell you I love you?"

Silence fell and lay heavily over the room for several seconds.

"Only if you mean it," Romy drawled.

Kit's heart started beating again, and he backed away from the cliff. "I love anyone who can cook like this," he said and took another bite. *Maybe it would be best if I just kept my mouth full.* "Is there any more coffee?"

"I can see your sisters have spoiled you," Romy said as he took the tray of toasted French bread from the oven. "The coffee's on the counter, and I'm sure you know where the cups are since this is your house."

"But I'm injured," Kit said in a piteous voice and then ruined the effect by laughing.

Romy set a plate of toast and the butter dish on the table and poured Kit a cup of coffee. "Don't get used to this," he said as he put the cup down next to Kit's hand.

"I won't." Kit beamed a smile at Romy. "And thank you."

"Aw, what the hell," Romy said. "I guess you can get used to it."

"I intend to spoil you, too," Kit warned. "So what should we do with the rest of the day?"

"I should go to the garage and install a radiator, but the customer doesn't need it until Wednesday. I'll have to work longer tomorrow, but if you want me to stay, I will."

"I'd like it if you never left." Kit polished his plate with a piece of bread as he spoke. "We could be roommates." Kit tossed the piece of toast into his mouth and chewed. "Doesn't that sound like fun?"

"Maybe we should try a few sleepovers first."

"That sounds like fun too." Kit sipped his coffee. "If you need to work, go ahead. Just because I'm stuck here all alone doesn't mean you have to stay with me."

"No, it's too late to change your mind now. I'm staying."

So Romy stayed and played video games with Kit, fetching whatever Kit needed, to save Kit from getting up and down too much. Though Kit didn't want to admit it, he was still very sore, and he was grateful for Romy's help, despite his complaints about being treated like a baby. A little after nine, Kit's last dose of pain meds put him to sleep in the middle of a sentence. Romy sat there for a while with his arm around Kit and Kit's head on his shoulder, while some brainless comedy played on the television, and he was perfectly content.

At ten, Romy eased Kit down to lie on the couch and put a pillow under his head. Pulling the soft blanket off the back of the couch, Romy spread it over Kit. He kissed Kit's forehead and left the apartment, turning off lights on the way to the door. The half-hour commute to the garage went by in the blink of an eye as Romy relived the moments he'd spent just sitting quietly with Kit leaning against him. He didn't feel like sleeping when he got home, so he went ahead and replaced the radiator on Mr. Johnson's sedan. Finally feeling tired enough to sleep, he went to bed.

THIRTEEN

ROMY WORKED hard all day Wednesday and spent most of Thursday at an auto-parts auction. He talked with Kit on the phone, but they didn't see each other until the weekend.

Kit drove to the garage at seven and informed Romy that his jaw was much better and he had a craving for something different. Romy took him to an outdoor cantina that served ice-cold beer and tequila. In the middle of a circle of wooden tables, an old lady with skin like a walnut cooked tortillas on a hot stone. Beside her, a second old lady grilled corn, poblano peppers, and strips of beef over open flames. A third elderly woman shuffled around delivering the food wrapped in corn husks.

"This is cool," Kit said as he sat down on a bench.

"I thought you might like it." Romy thanked the lady who poured shots for them and raised his glass in a toast to Kit before he drank.

"I like that you're modern and old-fashioned at the same time." Kit drank his tequila. "I'm just modern and boring."

"Boring? You?" Romy laughed and looked up to find the old lady at his elbow again. He nodded and she refilled the cups. "I haven't had a boring moment since I met you."

"Really?" Kit's face glowed as he looked across the table at Romy.

"It's exciting for me just sitting this close to you."

"I could listen to you all night." Kit smiled as a platter of loaded tortillas landed in the middle of the table followed by several small bowls of garnishes.

Both young men thanked the lady and got down to the business of eating. They shoveled in the delicious food, laughed with their mouths full, and drank a few ice-cold beers with lime. After leaving a generous amount of money on the table, they walked away talking about how full they were.

"I like this walking thing," Kit said. "Especially after a feast like that."

"I don't have a lot of choice, so I'm glad there are a lot of good places within walking distance of the garage."

They were approaching a bar with music pouring out the open door when Romy pulled Kit into an alley. "I've been wanting to do this," he said as he put an arm around Kit's waist and pulled him to his chest.

To the beat of the music from the bar, Romy began to dance, leading Kit in a slow waltz around the cramped space. Kit leaned his cheek against Romy's and swayed with him until the song was over.

"That was nice," Kit murmured, looking into Romy's eyes.

Romy looked up as someone passed by the mouth of the alley. "I hope I get to dance with you again soon," he said.

"Do you have music at your place?" Kit asked.

"As a matter of fact, I do. Good thinking." Romy pulled Kit out of the alley and they continued down the street.

They were talking about music to dance to when a car passed and someone yelled out the window. Kit froze with his eyes fixed on the taillights as the car slowed down.

"Are you okay?" Romy asked.

"Sure. I just had a bad moment. Kind of flashed back to the carjacking."

The car stopped and Kit tensed up, clenching his hands into fists.

"It's okay," Romy told Kit. "These aren't dirtbag delinquents out to bash some queers. And you're not alone."

Three guys got out of the car, and Kit was flooded with relief as he recognized the musicians from the club Romy had taken him to. Kit smiled as the trio greeted Romy warmly, hugging him exuberantly, and in one case, lifting him off the ground in a bear hug.

"Okay, Koda, let me breathe now," Romy said. "You guys remember Kit, right?"

"Who could forget Kit?" Joplin said. "Good to see you again."

"So what's up?" Romy asked. "Did you stop just to harass us?"

"Harsh, bro," Koda said. "It's The Heater's twenty-first birthday tomorrow so we're taking him out tonight. Want to join us?"

"We were just headed back to my place," Romy said. "Another time, okay?"

"Come on," Tommy Bernz aka The Heater said, tossing back his long hair. "You never go out with us anymore."

"He's right. You don't," Koda said, propping an arm on The Heater's shoulder.

"Come on," Joplin said. "We arranged a private party at Club Red. Tonight we own the place. It's going to be a gay Mardi Gras!"

"It sounds like fun," Kit said, looking at Romy. "Why don't we go for a little while?"

"Sure," Romy said. "Honestly, I'd hate to miss seeing The Heater blow his candles out."

When they got to the club, it was obvious that the party had been going on for some time. The Heater's arrival detonated a blast wave of cheers that reached all corners of the room. Drinks were raised in toast and a speech was demanded of the birthday boy.

The Heater was already staggering drunk, and he clutched Romy and Kit's forearms for support as he spoke. "I intend to kiss everyone at least once before the night is over," he announced and the crowd cheered again.

Kit turned to say something to Romy and found himself nose to nose with The Heater. The Heater grinned and grabbed Kit, kissing him thoroughly. When the kiss finally ended, and The Heater moved away looking for fresh victims, Kit fanned himself with his hand.

"I'd say he's been practicing," Kit told Romy as they watched The Heater grab someone else.

"Looks like it's going to be that kind of party," Romy said, as Koda reeled The Heater in by his wrist, bent him backward, and claimed his mouth as the crowd shouted encouragement, advice, and praise.

"That's hot," Kit said. He glanced at Romy. "So these are the people you hung out with before I came along?"

"Believe it or don't, these are my friends."

"And to think I was nervous that you'd find out about my party boy past." Kit looked around at the laughing, dancing crowd that showed every sign of evolving into an orgy. "I've got nothing on you."

"They're musicians." Romy shrugged. "They're supposed to act like that."

Kit smiled impishly. "But not you, right?"

"Of course not." Romy assumed a pious expression. "I'm a good boy."

"You're a good boy who knows when to be bad, and that's the best kind."

The DJ put on a slower song and Romy took Kit's hand. "Want to dance?"

Kit came into Romy's arms and moved with him like a shadow. Bodies pressed together, they let the melody and rhythm dictate their steps, let the music carry them like a magic carpet. They were lost in the sensation of hard muscles flexing under cloth, the tantalizing friction of fabric against skin, the alluring scents you could only smell when you were this close to someone. Unable to resist, Romy nuzzled at Kit's earlobe, sucking it briefly into his mouth. Kit turned his head and Romy's lips skidded across Kit's cheek to meet his mouth. They traded kisses as they danced in place, swaying slightly, oblivious to their surroundings until the kiss ended.

Kit's eyes sparkled as he looked into Romy's soft gaze. "Best kiss ever," he said.

"There *is* something very sexy about dancing and kissing at the same time. Maybe it reminds us of making love."

"We haven't made love yet," Kit reminded him.

"We've only been dating for a couple of weeks."

"True, but we're healthy young guys. We should've at least given each other hand jobs by now. Some guys would've been through the whole Kama Sutra."

"Really? You've seen the schedule?"

Kit laughed softly as he rubbed his nose against Romy's. "I *made* the schedule," he said.

Romy hugged Kit tightly. He opened his mouth to speak but a roar went up, and he and Kit turned to see what the commotion was.

From a rear door marched six muscular men dressed in nothing but thongs and gleaming oil. Between them, they carried an enormous cake shaped like the Eiffel Tower.

"The Heater's favorite monument," Romy whispered to Kit. "And not just because it's an enormous phallic symbol. He wants to go to Paris."

"Doesn't everyone?" Kit grinned at the look on The Heater's face when the bass player saw the cake. "I like your friends," he told Romy.

"They know how to party, that's for sure," Romy said, looking around. "Now I remember why I don't spend as much time with them as I used to."

Kit raised his eyebrows.

"The noise, the groping, the puking…." Romy let his voice trail off. "I just can't afford to stay up all night drinking anymore."

"It's fun once in a while. Except for the puking."

"Exactly."

"Was that a hint? Do you need to go home now?"

"I should," Romy said and then laughed when Koda and Joplin pushed The Heater's face into the cake. "But first, let's wish The Heater a happy birthday."

Kit and Romy had whipped cream all over their faces by the time they escaped The Heater's clutches. They were only too happy to help one another clean up in a dark corner before they went outside to look for a cab.

"What are you doing tomorrow night?" Kit asked as the taxi dropped them at the garage.

"I have no plans," Romy said, leaning against the hood of Kit's car.

"Want to have dinner with me and Ash? You can invite one of your friends if you want."

"I think I'll be fine without a chaperone." Romy smiled as he tilted Kit's face for a kiss. "Where should I meet you?"

"I'll send a car."

"You'll send a car?" Romy's lips moved against Kit's neck.

"If that's okay."

"Sure, why not?" Romy licked the divot between Kit's collarbones.

Kit shivered. "Man, if you knew what you do to me," he breathed.

Romy moaned as Kit squeezed his butt cheeks, parting them and kneading the firm muscles. He sucked at the sensitive skin of Kit's throat, flicking his tongue against the silky flesh. Kit gripped Romy's ass harder, pressing their crotches together. Each slippery pass of Romy's tongue over

Kit's skin jolted Kit's excitement up another notch. Pushing a knee between Romy's thighs, Kit pulsed his hips, rubbing his bulge against Romy's. Trapped between Kit and the Ferrari's fender, Romy didn't have much room to maneuver, so he settled for holding Kit tighter and pouring all his passion into the kiss. Both were so aroused they came in a matter of heartbeats.

"Fuck!" Romy breathed into Kit's mouth as his climax exploded and short-circuited all his systems. He collapsed onto the hood of the car, taking Kit with him.

Kit made a trail of little sucking kisses up Romy's throat as he enjoyed the slow roll of his orgasm receding. "Well, that didn't suck," he mumbled against the stubble-scratchy underside of Romy's chin.

Romy lifted his head, gave Kit a deadpan look, and then broke into laughter. Kit gathered Romy into his arms and pulled him up to sit on the fender.

"Are you okay with what just happened?" Kit asked, looking up at Romy.

Romy rested his forearms on Kit's shoulders and leaned his forehead against Kit's. "It was bound to happen sooner or later. Speaking for myself, it was fantastic."

"Really?" Kit grinned. "I mean, I know it was fantastic for me, but I'm glad you liked it too."

"*Like* is not the word I'd use."

"What word would you use?"

"Let me see," Romy drawled as the languor of afterglow crept through him. "I've already used *fantastic*. I guess I'd describe it as…. No, that doesn't begin to describe it. Would you take my word that it was the best thing I've ever felt?"

Kit tilted his chin, offering his mouth for a kiss. Romy cradled Kit's head between his hands and took Kit's lips in a slow, sweet kiss that neither wanted to end. Kit rested his arms on Romy's thighs, hands gripping Romy's hips, fingers sinking into lean muscles as a spasm of pure emotion gripped him. Unable to breathe, he broke the kiss.

"I love you," he gasped like a drowning man.

Romy pulled Kit's head to his chest and stroked his hair. "Do you feel like you were struck by lightning?" he murmured.

Kit nodded.

"Me too." Romy kissed Kit's forehead.

They stayed entwined for a while, just resting against one another in that sweet lull that is the legacy of a good climax. Neither wanted to move and break the spell, but eventually Romy went inside and Kit drove home. They were already missing each other before they were out of one another's sight.

Though Romy hadn't said he loved Kit, Kit was happy with Romy's response to his blurted declaration. At least he knew Romy felt the same way, even if Romy hadn't uttered the actual words. Of course, Kit was a little disappointed, but he also felt an unfamiliar calm, a sense that things would play out as they were meant to, and there was no point in being stressed. He knew he'd worry and waver anyway, but it was nice to feel this peace while it lasted.

Romy peeled off his jeans and underwear and dropped them in the laundry basket. He took a quick shower and went to bed, feeling pleasantly relaxed and satisfied. Despite all his reserve and good intentions, his relationship with Kit continued to hurtle forward like a rocket sled. But it felt so right that he didn't want to risk derailing it by throwing on the brakes. He should probably just stop trying to control it and let it take its course. Even if it ended with a crash, it was one hell of a ride.

FOURTEEN

"WOW," ROMY said as the gleaming limousine pulled into his parking lot. He locked the office and walked over as the driver got out. "Hat, boots, and everything," he said under his breath.

"Good evening, sir," the handsome chauffeur said as he opened the back door. "I'm Rocky. I hope you're having a good evening."

"It's getting better all the time," Romy said. He slid across the leather upholstery and the driver shut the door.

"There's a bar for your convenience," the chauffeur said as he got behind the wheel and buckled up. "The refrigerator is in the cabinet directly in front of you." He pulled out of the parking lot. "Feel free to ask me any questions as you enjoy the ride."

Romy took a bottle of sparkling water from the refrigerator and opened it. "Not bad," he said after taking a drink. "I still don't think it's worth five dollars a bottle, though."

The driver chuckled. "The scotch is a very good one, I hear."

"Not my poison," Romy said.

"It's all complimentary."

"I'm fine."

"Enjoy the ride then, sir."

Romy sat back and sipped his expensive water as they passed through increasingly luxurious neighborhoods. As Rocky pulled off the throughway, the limo coasted to a stop.

"Nothing to worry about. Just stay where you are, sir," Rocky said. "I'll call for help."

"Why don't we take a look under the hood first?"

"Look, I'm not really a chauffeur, okay? I'm an actor whose cousin is a chauffeur who sometimes lets me pick up cash by driving his car. I don't know a thing about engines."

Romy reached for the door handle and Rocky scrambled to get out of the car. "It's okay," Romy said as he walked around to the front. "Hit the hood latch for me." A few minutes later Romy called out. "Try the engine."

The limo started right up and Romy closed the hood.

"How'd you do that?" Rocky asked as he held the door for Romy.

"The battery cable had worked itself loose. Probably on the potholes in my neighborhood. You'll need to tighten it with a wrench or it'll happen again."

"Thanks," Rocky said. "You've got some grease on your hands, but I've got some wet wipes in the glove compartment."

Rocky got in and handed the packet of towelettes to Romy before fastening his seat belt.

"So you're really a mechanic?" he said as he pulled back onto the road. "I thought maybe the garage was a property you owned or something."

"I'm really a mechanic."

"That's cool. You just saved my butt."

"It was no big deal. So you're an actor?" Romy adroitly deflected the conversation.

Rocky was happy to talk about himself until he dropped Romy off at the restaurant. As he opened the door for Romy, he handed him a pager. "Just call when you're ready to go."

"Thanks," Romy said before he went into the restaurant.

Romy gave the hostess his name and was immediately shown to a table where Kit and Ash were already seated.

"I hope you like seafood," Ash said after Romy sat down. "This place is famous for crab."

"We've already opened a bottle of white, as you can see," Kit said. "Would you like some?"

"Maybe with dinner. Water's fine for now." Romy smiled. "I like you in black."

Kit turned to Ash. "You were right," he said.

"I told Kit to wear the black shirt." Ash leaned toward Romy as though confiding a secret. "I'm a genius."

"Well then, what do you think I should order for dinner?"

Ash smiled. "Oh, I like him, Kit. I really like him."

"Why don't you order for everyone?" Kit said as his foot touched Romy's under the table. "I've been set on vibrate since last night," he said softly as soon as Ash was absorbed in the menu.

"I'm not sure what that means, but I like the sound of it," Romy replied.

"It means I can't wait to get you alone so I can jump you."

"I know just how you feel." Romy smiled as Kit's foot caressed his calf. "But first dinner and then dessert."

"I'll try and control myself." Kit put his chin on his palm and gazed at Romy. "You look more handsome every time I see you."

"Well, at least we have that much in common." Romy gazed fondly back at Kit.

"Hey!" Ash snapped his fingers. "Absolutely not. The two of you are not allowed to drift off into fluffy sexitude. It's rude."

"You may have to remind us," Kit said.

"Perfect!" Ash said as he saw their server approaching. "Here comes some of that delicious, fresh-baked bread. Stuff your mouths with that for now." Ash gave the young man their order and the waiter departed. "Now, let's get acquainted," he said.

Romy good-naturedly allowed Ash to interview him as they enjoyed the bread and then the appetizers. When the main course arrived, conversation ceased as respect was given to the outstanding dishes.

"Good call," Kit told Ash as he wiped his mouth with his napkin.

"It was really delicious," Romy said.

"Now who wants to go and work some of it off?" Ash asked. "Mirrorball Palace just reopened. I know I can get us in the door."

"I was hoping to get Romy alone sometime soon," Kit said as they left the table.

"Understandable." Ash slipped into the jacket the coat-check valet held for him. "But you should probably get some exercise first." He tipped the valet and went to the door. "You don't want to hurt Romy, after all." Ash chuckled as the other two joined him.

"The club is so far away," Kit complained as they walked out onto the sidewalk.

"Yes, but you hired a limo, didn't you?" Ash grinned. "The party doesn't have to stop."

"That's true." Kit looked at Romy. "What do you say?"

"It's only a little after nine," Romy said.

"Wonderful!" Ash exclaimed. "Let's go."

During the ride to the club, Ash insisted on pouring shots every time they made it through a green light. By the time they stepped out of the car, the three men were more than slightly sozzled.

"Perfect," Ash declared.

"What's perfect?" Kit asked as a bouncer stepped in front of him.

"We are in the perfect condition for this club." Ash faced the bouncer, pulling out his wallet as he began talking. In another minute, the door was opened and Kit, Romy, and Ash walked into a maelstrom of light and noise. Ash turned his head from side to side like a hound casting for a scent and then pointed.

"There's a table. Let's hustle."

With Ash leading the way, the trio snowplowed their way through the dense crowd and claimed the small table. There were only two chairs, but they considered themselves lucky.

"We'll never get any service," Kit said. "I'm going to the bar to order drinks."

As soon as Kit moved away, Ash began asking Romy questions. "So what's the story with you and Kit?"

"We're dating."

"Yes, obviously you're dating, but tell me more."

"Ummm...."

"Look, I've known Kit a long time and I've seen him date a lot of guys, but I've never seen him act like this."

"Like what?"

"He's just so... *happy*."

"He wasn't happy before?"

"Well, naturally he was happy sometimes, but it was this total like manic thing. One night he'd be dancing on the bar, drinking everyone under the table, and snaking the hottest guys, and the next day, he'd be all mopey. He'd go out, but he'd just sit there and drink all night. Now, he seems genuinely happy. You must be good for him."

"I hope so." Romy smiled as he watched Kit at the bar. "He sure makes me happy."

"I like you, Romy O'Keefe."

"Good. I hear you're Kit's oldest friend, and I'd like you to be my friend too."

"A pleasure," Ash said. "It's so good to see Kit happy. I thought he was never going to get over...." He paused and started again. "As you may have noticed, Kit is rather attractive, and in some circles, considered a real prize."

"I can imagine, but I don't think of him that way."

Ash looked into Romy's eyes as he spoke. "You sound sincere," he said. "More importantly, you don't sound like a guy who's so deep in the closet he found Narnia."

"I'm not exactly wearing a Gay Pride T-shirt either." Romy smiled at Ash. "Look, I like Kit, okay? He makes life fun for me. I plan to be around him as much as possible. Other than that, I have no agenda."

"Then I guess you don't get to hear my speech about how I'd kick your ass if you hurt Kissy. Or actually, how I'd hire a couple of big guys to kick your ass." Ash looked around as someone jostled his chair. "It's really crowded in here tonight."

"I thought it was just me. I'm starting to feel a little claustrophobic."

"I apologize. I'm the one who insisted on coming here."

"So it's your fault so many people came here tonight?"

Ash smiled. "It's possible."

Kit came back and stood between Romy and Ash. "It makes me so happy to see you two getting along," he said.

"We were just talking about running away together when you came back," Ash said.

Kit pretended to punch Ash. "Don't even joke about that," he said.

"Babe," Romy said. "He wasn't joking."

"Oh, shit," Kit said. "I should never have introduced the two of you."

Everyone laughed just as a waiter appeared with their drinks. "Good to see people having a good time," the waiter said. "As you can tell, it's a zoo in here tonight, but I'll try to get back by your table."

"Thanks." Kit gave the young man a handful of money. "In case we don't see you again," he said.

The waiter looked at the bills before putting them in his pocket. "Oh, you'll see me again," he said before he was swallowed by the crowd.

"Scooch," Kit said and perched a butt cheek on the corner of Romy's chair.

Romy slid over a bit. "So this is an uptown gay bar," he said.

"Not strictly speaking," Ash said. "But pretty much anything goes."

"Good to know." Romy wrapped an arm around Kit to help him stay on the chair but mostly just because he could and it felt good.

Kit turned his head and kissed Romy.

"I guess I can say good-bye to my playmate." Ash pretended to wipe away a tear.

"What are you talking about?" Kit said.

"Well, it's obvious to me that you're severely smitten with Mr. Slim Sultry here with the enchanting bedroom eyes and even more enchanting bedroom voice, so I need to either find a new comrade in corruption, or get used to spending my evenings alone watching chick flicks and washing down popcorn with white wine."

"Kit can go out with his friends anytime he wants to," Romy said.

"But he doesn't want to, does he, Kissy?"

Kit didn't even pretend he wasn't delighted to be the subject of the conversation. "No, I don't. The thought of going out for a wild night of boozing and hitting on hotties doesn't appeal to me at all now."

"Admit it," Ash said with feigned disgust. "You don't want to do anything that doesn't involve Romy."

"I can't deny it." Kit put a hand over Romy's where it rested on his hip. "I have a massive crush. I just want to be with him all the time."

"It works for me," Romy said dryly.

"Fuck me!" Ash exclaimed loudly, startling his companions and several people nearby.

"What?" Kit said.

"I'm so jealous." Ash looked from Kit to Romy and back. "I'm serious. I totally envy you guys. Just look at the two of you beaming love and joy at the universe. It's a little sickening, but truly, I'm so jealous I could tease my hair."

The waiter came back with fresh drinks, though they hadn't ordered anything. "Compliments of the management," he said, nodding toward the mezzanine that encircled the room. A handsome man in a dark suit smiled at Ash. "Mr. del Toro would like to meet you," the waiter said.

Ash looked at Romy and Kit.

"You can bail on us if you want," Kit said. "I would."

"You're an angel," Ash said. "And yon manager type is *so* hot."

"Good luck," Romy said.

"I think you two already brought me good luck," Ash said as he stood.

"Call me tomorrow," Kit said. He turned to Romy, "Speaking of luck...."

"Looks like we're on our own," Romy said as Ash followed the waiter.

"All alone with a limo." Kit smirked at Romy. "We shouldn't let it go to waste."

"What did you have in mind?"

Kit whispered in Romy's ear.

"I could go for that," Romy said. "You want to finish your drink?"

Kit got up and pulled Romy to his feet. "If I want booze, there's more in the limo. Let's go."

Romy paged the driver, and the car was at the curb near the corner when he and Kit finally fought their way out of the club.

"Jesus, I lost count of how many times I was groped," Kit said as they walked to the limo.

"How about the number of hard-ons that rubbed on you?"

"It *was* fun, wasn't it?" Kit laughed.

"And kind of scary. If one of us had slipped and fallen, who knows what might have happened." Romy nodded at the driver as he opened the limo door.

Kit slid in and Romy got in after him. The driver closed the door and walked around to get in behind the wheel.

"Where would you like to go, sirs?" he said.

"Could you just drive around for a while?" Kit said. "We want to have a few drinks and look at the lights."

"No problem. I know a route that'll take us past the best neon in the city."

"Outstanding." Kit opened the bar. "Holy hell, look at this bottle of brandy!"

"Is it a good one?"

"Uh, yeah, you might say that." Kit poured a couple of fingers into two crystal tumblers and handed one to Romy. "Driver, could we have privacy, please?"

The panel between the front and the rear slid smoothly up with hardly a sound.

Romy held the glass under his nose. "Smells strong."

"Yeah, you might say that, too." Kit rolled the rim of the glass against his lips. "I'm really glad we found each other."

"So am I. I always have such a good time with you."

"And to think we wouldn't have met if my fuel filter hadn't clogged up."

"Thank God for ants in their multitudes."

Kit snickered. "What's that word?" he asked. "The one that means finding what you need by pure accident?"

"Um, destiny?"

"No, destiny happens on purpose. The word I'm thinking of sounds weirder." Kit thought for a few seconds. "Why can't I come up with it? My mom used to say it to me all the time."

"Is it important?"

"It's just that it's the perfect word to describe how we got together. Someday, we might have a yacht, and we'll need a name for it."

"Lunatic."

"Serendipity!"

"Is that the word or are you cursing me in Italian?"

"That's the word. And it's not Italian. It was made up by some English writer back in the day. Okay, we can drink now." Kit held up his glass. "To serendipity."

Kit watched as Romy put the glass to his lips and took a sip. "Good?"

"It's burny, but yeah, it's good."

Kit wet his lips with the brandy and set the glass down. Leaning toward Romy, he looked into Romy's eyes, letting his desire for him pour out. Romy put a hand on Kit's cheek and brought their mouths together in a melting kiss. Kit turned sideways and put a knee on the seat, resting his hands on Romy's shoulders as he deepened the kiss. Romy's tongue accepted the invitation to stray and thoroughly explored the soft wetness of Kit's mouth.

When the kiss ended, Romy licked his lips. "I love the way you taste," he said.

Kit knelt on the seat, straddling Romy's thighs, and took his mouth in another groin-tightening kiss. Romy pulled the tails of Kit's shirt out of his pants and slid his hands up Kit's back, caressing the smooth skin over the hard muscles. Kit moaned when Romy bit at his nipples, making them draw up and sucking them into his mouth. Letting go of Romy's shoulders, Kit swiftly unbuttoned his shirt to give Romy more access. Romy showed his gratitude for the help by teasing Kit's nipples until Kit was half-delirious with pleasure. Putting his hands on Kit's hips, he urged him up until they were face to crotch. Romy rubbed his face over the bulge in Kit's trousers, taking little nips at the curved ridge.

"You're driving me crazy," Kit whispered breathlessly.

Romy unzipped Kit's pants and drew his hard cock out through the opening. Kit's breath hissed through his clenched teeth as Romy's lips touched the head of his shaft.

"Hang on," Kit said. "I can't reach you."

"Just let me do what I want for now, okay?" Romy looked up into Kit's liquid gaze.

Kit bit his lip and braced his palms against the limo's ceiling as Romy took him in his mouth. The hot wetness felt amazing on his taut flesh. It both soothed and exacerbated the tantalizing itch. "Damn, that feels so good," Kit moaned.

Romy hummed his thanks and Kit moaned again. Praying that the privacy panel had some kind of soundproofing, Romy took Kit's full length until he felt the head nudge the back of his throat. He applied suction, hollowing his cheeks as he drew back, and felt Kit tremble under his hands. A wave of exultation swept him up, making him tremble as well. His fingers sank into the hard muscles of Kit's ass as he pulled Kit forward, taking him deeper, sucking harder, teasing with his tongue and teeth.

Kit reached down to tangle his fingers in Romy's hair, letting the thick strands slide over his skin, as he sought something to hold onto. His excitement had reached a dizzying peak and he was afraid that if he wasn't anchored, he'd just go flying off like an unknotted balloon. It was just too much that he was getting a blow job in the back of a limo with the driver mere feet away, but it was so much more than that. It was the fact that Romy was the one lavishing attention on his cock that really sent him into orbit. Torn between the intense desire to touch Romy more intimately and the selfish inclination to just enjoy what Romy was doing, Kit decided to leave it up to Romy.

Romy was deeply into his current venture, immersed in the textures and scents and the sounds that Kit made as he caressed him. It had been a long time since he'd taken such pleasure in giving pleasure and he lost himself in it, forgetting where he was, taking no notice of anything beyond the feel of smooth skin and crisp hair, the smells of musk and soap. He heard nothing but the moans, gasps, and small cries he drew from Kit. His hard cock pulsed in time with Kit's labored breathing, and he reached down to cup his crotch with one hand. As he bobbed his head, he massaged himself to the same rhythm.

Acting on pure instinct now, Kit flexed his thigh muscles and thrust into Romy's mouth. Romy sucked harder, pressing his tongue to the wide vein on the underside of Kit's cock. Kit rolled his hips slowly, moving like a man underwater, drowning in bliss. Romy looked up and saw Kit looking down at him. Their eyes met and held and a slow smile spread over Kit's face. Romy groaned as his climax hit him and he rode out the warm wave, holding tightly to his cock until it stopped jerking. Kit's cock seemed to thicken in Romy's mouth, and Kit's thigh muscles quivered as he abruptly stopped thrusting. Romy grasped Kit's butt cheeks and squeezed as he tightened his lips and slid them down Kit's dick to the root. He ignored the prickly tickle of pubic hair as he hummed and swallowed until Kit bucked against him.

"Holy fucking hell," Kit said breathlessly as he came. His fingers tightened on a fistful of Romy's tangled mane as he spurted down Romy's throat. Gently, he rocked against Romy as the powerful orgasm rushed through him and receded in a series of groin-tightening aftershocks.

Romy swallowed a final time, and let Kit's cock slide from his mouth. He looked up into Kit's pleasure-glazed eyes with a serious expression.

"My first limo blow job," Romy said. "So how was it?"

Kit smiled and kissed Romy. *Thank God, it wasn't going to be weird or awkward now.* "It was off the charts," he said softly, his nose bumping Romy's. "There's no scale that goes high enough. It was…." He smiled again. "It was without a doubt the best head I've ever gotten from a mechanic in a limousine."

"Asshole."

Kit chuckled as he sank down until he was sitting between Romy's legs. "And now it's my turn."

"Uh, I already got off. You couldn't tell?"

"My loss." Kit rubbed the crotch of Romy's jeans. "But you're not home yet."

An hour later, Kit got out of the limo at his apartment. "Don't forget about the barbecue," he said as he stuck his head back in the car. He wanted to kiss Romy good night, but the chauffeur was standing right next to him waiting to close the door. As if the thought was a Jedi mind trick, the driver turned his back and took out his phone. Kit leaned in and gave Romy a kiss that conveyed just how much he'd enjoyed the evening. "See you tomorrow."

Romy watched Kit go into the building as the limo pulled away from the curb. He thought the date could be considered a success. Happily, he chatted with the driver until he was dropped off at the garage.

FIFTEEN

"I'M NOT sure this is a good idea," Romy said as he buttoned his shirt. It felt a little weird putting on someone else's clothes in someone else's bedroom, but when Kit had asked if he wanted to borrow something, Romy had jumped at the offer. He couldn't think of a thing he owned that was suitable for a millionaire's barbecue.

"You're not backing out now." Kit looked over at his boyfriend and turned away from the mirror. "It'll be fine. I promise I won't leave you alone with any of my family members. And if any of them start eyeing you like you're a juicy steak, I'll shoot them with silver bullets."

"I'm still a little nervous."

"I think that's normal, but I could blow you again if you think it'd help."

"Couldn't hurt," Romy said. "But seriously, between last night and the two times you've made me come since I got here, I think I'm sexed out for now.

Kit stepped back and looked Romy over. "I told you we were the same size," he said. "I'll bet we're about the same weight, too. We're just shaped a little differently."

Romy turned to the mirror. The black linen trousers and jacket and cream-colored T-shirt fit him perfectly and were an attractive blend of casual and stylish. "I could get used to this."

"You look yummy," Kit said. "I wish I really did have time to eat you."

"Why don't you save it as a reward if I do well?"

"Baby, blowing you is *my* reward."

In the middle of an indulgent smile, something occurred to Romy. "How did we get here?" he mused.

Kit looked up from threading a belt through the loops of Romy's waistband. "You took a cab to my place. I live here, so…."

"No, I mean how did we get to this place where we're so comfortable with each other in just a few weeks?"

"Let's not analyze it."

"Okay." Romy chuckled. "I remember my first reaction to you. *What's this precious pretty-boy doing in my grungy garage?*"

"Not exactly flattering."

"Well, I did think you were gorgeous."

"That's a little better."

"And sexy."

"Much better." Kit went to his dresser and picked up his brush.

"And then I thought, there's an angel standing there on the oil stains."

Kit smiled at his reflection in the mirror. "Hardly an angel."

"Well, you looked like one. Truthfully, I have to readjust my impression of you every two minutes."

"Is that good?"

"Well, it isn't boring."

"Then it's good." Kit paused in brushing his hair. "I think. I guess hurricanes aren't boring either."

Romy chuckled. "You may be a force of nature, but you're not a natural disaster."

"Really? Could you explain that to my parents?" Kit laughed when Romy's expression changed suddenly. "I'm kidding, silly. All you have to say to them is 'hi' and 'thanks for inviting me.' It'll be easy. We'll walk around my sister's humungous backyard, eat some barbecue, mingle a little, and come home to fuck like minks."

"I'll just keep reminding myself that your mom and dad will see me as your friend and not someone who's sexing up their baby boy on a regular basis."

"Not regular enough."

"No?" Romy came to stand behind Kit, wrapping his arms around Kit's trim waist. "What would be enough?"

"It could never be enough, but as long as you're asking, at least once an hour would keep me from having cravings."

Romy kissed Kit's nape. "We'd have to move closer to each other."

"I'm willing to make the sacrifice. Are there any places for sale or rent near you?"

"You really are a lunatic." Romy gave Kit a squeeze before letting him go.

"Just because I'd move to be closer to you?"

"Most people would just deal with the reality of not being able to give up a place they can afford that's reasonably near where they work. Not to mention what a hassle moving is."

"I'm not a big fan of reality." Kit brought his face close to Romy's, focusing his gaze on Romy's mouth as he continued, his breath caressing Romy's cheek. "I like living in my little dream world." He kissed the corner of Romy's lips. "And I'd like you to live there with me."

"Until I make my fortune, I'm afraid the best I can do is day trips."

Kit frowned, and Romy kissed him before speaking again.

"You can afford to buy or rent any place you want and hire people to move your stuff for you. It's not like that for me."

"I know that. And I'm not going to let it stop me from moving if I want to." Kit ran the pad of his thumb over Romy's bottom lip. "I'm not asking you to move, am I?"

Romy shook his head. "I'm not trying to start a fight," he said. "I'm just nervous about going to this rich-people party and meeting my boyfriend's family."

"I keep telling you, you'll be fine. They're just human beings."

"How could mere humans have produced something as perfect as you?"

Kit made a dismissive noise, but his lips curved in a pleased smile as he kissed Romy again. "We should probably leave now," he said reluctantly. He took a step back and held his arms out from his sides. "How do I look?"

"This is the first time I've seen you toned down. It's different, a little conventional, like you belong on a yacht, but you look very handsome."

Kit brushed his hands down his baby-blue broadcloth shirt. "Perfect," he said.

"So why did you tone down?"

"It's so lame, but I do it for my mom and dad, out of respect, I guess."

"I don't think that's lame."

"That's because you have character."

"You *are* a character," Romy said as he followed Kit out of the apartment.

Kit laughed. "We just had another one of those comfortable moments." He pushed the elevator button. "I love how we can go back and forth between deep stuff and cracking jokes."

"Laughing is good," Romy said as the elevator arrived. "Laughing with you is the best."

Kit pulled Romy into the elevator and kissed him. The kiss lasted until the doors opened on the ground floor. Kit's car was waiting at the curb, and in minutes, they were on the road, headed for Eliza's house in the suburbs.

"Wow," Romy said as they drove into Eliza's neighborhood in Clear Lake.

The houses here were set well back from the street with long sloping lawns, circular drives, and ornate fences. Most were two and three stories high with the occasional sprawling split-level. Eliza's house sat on five acres and had a man-made pond in the backyard. Introductions began as Kit and Romy walked around the house. By the time they reached the back, Romy had met two sisters and their families. When they got to the deck, they were greeted by Ash and another young man—introduced as Teddy Fonteyn—who hugged Kit warmly. After a few minutes of catching up, Kit pulled Romy away to meet his parents.

Mrs. Britten got up from a deck chair to hug her son, but Mr. Britten remained seated with his left leg propped on a padded footstool.

"How are you, Dad?" Kit asked.

"His leg's bothering him," Mrs. Britten said. She stayed standing with an arm around her son's waist, and it was obvious that she doted on him.

"It's not bad," Mr. Britten said. "You know how your mother fusses."

Kit smiled. "I'd like to introduce you to my friend," he said. "This is Romy O'Keefe."

"I don't recall hearing the name before," Mr. Britten said. "Did you go to college with Kit?"

"No, sir," Romy said. "I haven't been to college, but I hope to go someday."

"You went straight into the workforce, did you?" Mr. Britten said. "I like a man with ambition."

"Romy has plenty of that," Kit said.

"And so handsome," Mrs. Britten said. "Romy, you must have no trouble finding girlfriends."

"Maybe he can teach Kit," Mr. Britten said. "My son seems to be allergic to women."

"Dad!" Jules exclaimed as she came out to the deck carrying a cup of herbal tea. "You promised you wouldn't embarrass Kit today. Eliza doesn't want anything to mess up her barbecue."

"What did I say?" Mr. Britten took the cup.

"Kit has plenty of time to find a wife," Jules said. "Now drink your tea. It'll make you feel better."

"Plenty of time?" Mrs. Britten repeated. "Kit is twenty-four."

"Mom, have you thought that maybe Kit just isn't ready to get married?"

Mr. Britten snorted. "If people waited until they were ready, no one would get married."

Romy ducked his head to hide a smile as Kit spoke. "I haven't met a girl I want to marry."

"You should have a look around at this party," Mrs. Britten said. "There are a lot of young, pretty, suitable girls here."

"Most of them are related to me."

"Don't be unpleasant, dear," Mrs. Britten said.

"Sorry, Mom." Kit glanced at Romy. "I guess I should get out there and inspect the breeding stock."

Mrs. Britten gasped and Mr. Britten gave his son a sharp look.

"Sorry again," Kit said. He kissed his mom's cheek, promised to come to dinner soon, and made his escape with Romy. "Well, that was relatively painless," he said as they joined Ash and Teddy.

"Did your Mom and Dad give you a hard time about getting married?" Teddy asked.

"As always," Kit said.

"Someday they're going to show up at your house with a priest, a giant cake, and a nubile debutante," Ash said. "Unless you do something first."

"I know I've got to tell them," Kit said. "I just need to figure out the best way."

"What did you say?" Ash made a show of checking to see if Kit had a fever. "It sounded like something sensible."

"I can't take the pressure much longer," Kit said. "I thought when my sisters started having kids my folks would ease up on me, but they really want me to carry on the family name. It's like this ridiculous obsession with them. I mean, what's the difference? My sisters all have the same blood in their veins as I do. Why's the name so important?"

"I couldn't tell you," Ash said. He looked around at Kit, Romy, and Teddy. "It's almost like the Fabulous Four together again."

"Why isn't Parker here?" Teddy asked as he pushed his glasses up on his nose. "Your sister usually invites him to this bash."

"He's here somewhere," Ash said. "Why don't you go find him?"

"Fuck you, I think I will. See you later." Teddy walked away, almost colliding with a waiter carrying a tray of full glasses.

The waiter deftly avoided Teddy and offered the tray to Kit and his friends.

"Thanks," Romy said as he took a glass of lemonade.

Kit took a glass and the waiter moved away.

"Whoa!" Romy said after taking a sip. "There's a little lemonade in this vodka."

"It's good, isn't it?" Ash said.

"Yeah, I just didn't expect it."

"I should've warned you," Kit said. "This is Eliza's famous Yellow Fever. It's basically lemonade with lots of vodka, but she's proud of it, so...."

"So it's always served at her annual barbecue," Ash finished for Kit.

A little girl in a bright orange dress ran up to Kit and tugged at his trouser leg. He went down on one knee, and she whispered in his ear. Kit took her hand as he stood up.

"Time for the family picture," he said. "My niece is shy about talking in front of handsome men because she thinks her voice is sneaky."

"Squeaky!" the little girl corrected.

"It doesn't sound squeaky to me," Romy said.

The little girl giggled and smiled at Romy before leading Kit away. Kit looked over his shoulder at Romy. "I'll be back soon," he said. "You'll be safe with Ash."

"That's what you think," Ash said as Kit walked away.

"How did your evening go after Kit and I left?" Romy asked, already missing Kit.

"Quite well. Danny del Toro is what you call a smooth operator, and he's very interested in me. I'm seeing him later tonight—or tomorrow morning, to be precise."

"Good. It's not always easy to meet someone you want to spend time with."

"Yeah, like, what if Kit's car hadn't broken down?"

"I'd be a lonely man working sixteen hours a day."

"Thank Barbra fate stepped in. Why don't you come with me and I'll introduce you to some people who knew Kit while he was growing up? Won't that be fun?"

"Will I hear embarrassing stories about Kit?"

"Of course. That's the whole point."

Ash and Romy wandered around the big yard, stopping now and then when Ash saw someone he deemed worthy of speaking to. Romy sipped at his drink and filed the stories away for future use. Nearly an hour later, they were standing with the other two members of the erstwhile Fabulous Four, reminiscing about high school.

Romy glanced away and saw Kit talking to a man who defined tall, handsome, and well-groomed. They stood apart from the rest of the guests, near the pond at the far end of the lawn. Something in the stranger's posture unsettled Romy.

Ash noticed the direction of Romy's stare. "Well, I'll be damned," he said. "Look who's back from Tokyo."

"Who's the guy with Kit?"

"That's Brandis Young," Ash said. "He's Kit's ex."

Romy reacted to Ash's tone of voice. "Should I be worried?"

"Hm, Brandis claims to be straight these days. He even got married. But he does have a hungry look in his eyes, doesn't he?"

"Excuse me." Romy left Ash and walked over to stand next to Kit.

"Romy!" Kit exclaimed. "Let me introduce Brandis Young. Brandis, this is my good friend, Romy O'Keefe."

Brandis gave Romy a curt nod. "Romy O'Keefe," he said. "I don't think I've heard that name before."

"Doesn't surprise me," Romy said. "I doubt we travel in the same circles."

"So you're Kissy's *good* friend." Brandis glanced at the fading bruise on Kit's jaw. "I see you're taking good care of him."

"I can take care of myself," Kit said. "I'm a grown man."

"Of course you are." Brandis smiled, and Romy wanted to remove the smile with a car bumper at about seventy miles per hour. "Still working for your sister?"

"Stop it." Kit lowered his voice. "Can't we act like mature people?"

"You can try, but I don't think you'll convince anyone," Brandis said. "Sorry. That one just slipped out." He took a drink of his spiked lemonade. "You know, if you ever want to get serious about a career, I'd be happy to give you a position at my company."

"That's very generous of you," Kit said. "But I'm happy where I am."

"Are you?" Brandis took another sip of his drink. "I find that hard to believe. I could never be happy with scraps thrown to me by family."

"I'm not you."

Brandis glanced at Romy and then turned his gaze back to Kit. "Out of fairness to your friend, we probably shouldn't have this private conversation in front of him," he said.

"Why not?" Romy replied calmly, hiding his dismay at how easily Brandis had provoked him. "I don't know you, and whatever was between you and Kit is in the past. You can say what you need to say without being afraid you'll hurt my feelings."

"I'd rather have this talk with Kit in private."

"Well, that's a different situation," Romy said. "If you want me to leave, just say so."

"*I* don't want you to leave," Kit said.

Romy shrugged at Brandis. "Kit wants me to stay," he said.

"Fine." Brandis met Kit's eyes. "We have a lot of history," he said, his light, pleasant voice taking on the cadence of a rehearsed speech. "Some of it was good, and some of it was bad. Looking back, I can see now that I deserve some of the blame for the break-up. I was an arrogant, overbearing ass, and I'm sorry I hurt you. I'm sorry I was so obnoxious that you couldn't stand living with me. You're the best thing that's ever happened to me, and if you were mine again, I'd never treat you that way."

Kit stared at Brandis for several moments. "I accept your apology," he said at last.

"That's very gracious, but it wasn't so much an apology as a proposal."

"I don't understand." Kit narrowed his eyes in suspicion.

"I want you back. Wasn't that clear?"

"No, because never in a million years would I imagine that you'd have the colossal nerve or stupidity to think I'd get back on that horse."

"I guess I'll have to convince you, then."

"Hey," Romy broke in. "I'm not normally the kind of guy to go all caveman on you, but you're crossing a line here. Kit's with me."

"You had your chance to walk away," Brandis said. "I warned you."

"You're the one who should walk away," Kit told Brandis.

"You won't even hear my proposal?"

"There's no point," Kit said.

"Are you sure?" Brandis softened his tone. "Don't you remember how good we were together? I know you haven't forgotten Paris. That third-floor apartment we rented that didn't have an elevator? The little black-and-white cat that came in the window and ate the brie you left on the counter? The old lady at the corner shop who gave you a flower every morning?"

"Those are good memories," Kit said. "But that's all they are."

"We can make even better ones. I'm making a lot of money, in case you hadn't noticed, and the two years I just spent in Japan are going to make me so incredibly rich even I can't believe how rich I'm going to be."

"I don't really care about—" Kit broke off in midsentence as Eliza joined them.

"What are you all doing over here by yourselves?" Eliza asked. "The party's over there."

"We didn't mean to be rude," Kit said.

"You're forgiven," Eliza said. "Hello, Brandis. I'm so glad you could come. Mom and Dad would love to say hello to you."

"Thanks for inviting my family. I'll be sure and say hi. I miss my talks with Mr. Britten. He gave me a lot of great advice."

"He's very proud of the way you've built up your company, and you know Mom just adores you." Eliza looked around. "Where's Katrina?"

"My wife went off to gossip with Jules and Caroline," Brandis said. "You know what a social butterfly she is."

"How's Caroline doing?" Eliza asked.

"Can you believe my airhead little sister is graduating in the top twenty of her university?"

"I'll remember to congratulate her. She must have—"

"Would you excuse us?" Kit broke into the conversation. "Romy and I haven't eaten yet."

"What?" Eliza pretended outrage. "You haven't had any of my delicious food yet? I slaved for hours on the phone with the caterers. Get over there and stuff yourselves right now."

"I'm glad to you meet you, Romy O'Keefe," Brandis said. "Kit, I'll call you about that proposal."

"What's this?" Eliza perked up. "What are you boys plotting?" She patted Kit's arm. "If Brandis offers you a business deal, you should take it. He's got the golden touch."

"Let's not talk business," Kit said. "This is a party, right?"

Kit walked toward the buffet tables, taking Romy with him. "I'm not really hungry," he said. "I just had to get away."

"It *was* a little awkward."

"I can't believe no one told me Brand was back." Kit sighed. "Okay, I'm not going to let this ruin the whole day. The weather is perfect, and I'm with the perfect man."

Romy made a show of looking around for this so-called perfect man.

"I'm talking about you." Kit shook his head. "You're so silly sometimes."

"Perfection is hard to maintain. Sometimes I lapse."

"Come here." Kit hooked a finger in Romy's belt loop and pulled him behind one of the catering tents. Covering Romy's lips with his, Kit kissed him, trying to convey how he felt without words.

"Wow," Romy said when the kiss ended. "What did I do to deserve that?"

"*Kit's with me*," Kit quoted, dropping his voice a half octave.

"Sorry if I embarrassed you." Romy stroked Kit's cheek and let his hand rest on Kit's shoulder. "Are you okay?"

"I'm with you. Of course, I'm okay. And you didn't embarrass me, Brand did."

"Thanks. I was feeling a little insecure back there."

"I sure as hell couldn't tell."

"Well, I had to maintain my macho image. Your ex is kind of intimidating, if you hadn't noticed."

"Could you not call him my ex? And yeah, now that you mention it, he can be intimidating. But I noticed he didn't make you back down."

"Well, you know how it is when the alpha-male gene kicks in."

"Cute. If you're ready to go, I think we've stayed long enough to be polite, and honestly, I don't want to walk around wondering when I'm going to bump into Brand again."

"It's not high on my list either."

"If we just keep walking across the side yard, we can duck into the trees and double back to where the car's parked."

"Sometimes I wonder if I should be worried about your flair for covert activities." Romy smiled. "And other times, I'm just thankful that I'll have a great partner when the zombie apocalypse comes."

Kit laughed. "I keep falling more in love with you every day."

Romy put an arm around Kit as they reached the trees. "Well, that's another thing we've got in common."

"No time to talk," Kit said, before he got choked up. "Come with me if you want to live."

Kit grabbed Romy's hand and pulled him into a run. They started laughing at the absurdity of two grown men running like fourth graders from imaginary enemies, and they were breathless when they reached the car. Still pretending they were being chased by undead assassins, Kit hurriedly unlocked the car and slid behind the wheel. Romy jumped in beside him, and Kit was giggling so hard he was stabbing at the start button and missing. Finally, Romy reached over and pushed it.

"Let's go back to my place so I can get you out of those clothes," Kit said as he stepped on the gas. Driving like the lunatic Romy had dubbed him, Kit made it to his apartment from his sister's house in record time. "And that was a personal best," Kit said as he parked the car. "Now let's go inside and try for another one."

Though Kit was in a hurry, he stopped at the door to say good evening to Mr. Martinez. Mr. Martinez wished the young men a good night's rest and they went inside. The elevator ride was a mélange of lips, tongues, hands, and the delicious friction of skin on skin. Tingling with anticipation, they all but sprinted down the hall to Kit's apartment. Once inside, they threw their arms around each other, lips meeting in a sweet collision that clicked their teeth together. They reeled out of the foyer, rocking from foot to foot in the preliminary steps of the world's oldest dance.

In the living room, Kit shoved Romy up against the wall and yanked his trousers down. He dove on Romy's handsome cock, licking, sucking, and nibbling. Delicately, he lapped at the liquid that oozed from the tip as he shuttled his hand up and down the spit-slippery shaft. Taking the head in his mouth again, he sucked steadily while dragging his tongue up, over, and around the taut knob. He felt it swell against the roof of his mouth and swallowed. He swallowed again, drinking down the bittersweet fluid as it hit the back of his throat. Softly, he continued to suck until he'd drained the last dribble of come.

Romy let out a long breath and raised his face from the crook of his arm. Letting the arm drop to his side, he slid down the wall until he faced Kit. He took Kit's head between his hands and pulled him into a passionate kiss. As he drew back, he met Kit's eyes and held them.

"I love you," he said. "Sorry I couldn't say it before."

"Well." Kit said in a shaky voice. "A good blow job will do that to you."

"Then get those pants down, mister."

Kit laughed softly as he stroked the triangle of skin left bare by Romy's collar. "I'm trying not to burst into tears like a big ol' sissy," he said. "I guess this means we're going steady."

Romy nuzzled Kit's ear. "Why fight it?" he murmured as he fondled Kit's hard-on. "Let's get these pants down."

"Hang on." Kit grabbed Romy's wrist.

"Why?" A crease appeared between Romy's dark eyebrows.

"I want you inside me the next time I come."

Romy swallowed. "I'm game," he said. "Just give me a few minutes to get my breath back." He looked down at his sated cock.

"Not a problem. Come with me," Kit said as he walked toward the bedroom.

Romy pulled up his pants and followed. He sat on the bed and watched Kit take various items from the top drawer of his dresser. When Kit put everything on the night table, Romy took a closer look.

"Lube and condoms," Kit said as he took off his clothes and draped them over the back of a chair. "Some of the lube is flavored. I thought I'd give you a choice." He climbed onto the bed and propped himself on the pillows with legs sprawled wide.

"Whichever is your favorite," Romy said. He stood and took off his jacket and T-shirt, putting them with Kit's clothes.

"Stop," Kit said as Romy unzipped. "Keep the pants on for now."

"Whatever you want," Romy said. He sat back down to take off his boots and socks and roll a condom on his dick, which stuck out of his fly.

"I want you to use this on me, and then I want you to put your cock in me."

"Works for me," Romy said, as he caught the bottle Kit tossed at him. He felt nowhere near as cool as he tried to sound. It had been over two years since he'd done this, and while he was pretty sure he remembered how, he was a little worried about his performance. More than anything, he wanted Kit to enjoy this and not decide to dump him for being physically incompatible. Those were two words he never wanted to hear spoken together again.

Romy looked up from the label on the bottle of lube and his breath caught in his throat at the sight of Kit lying on the bed waiting for him. His gaze followed the sleek lines of Kit's lithe, well-defined muscles along the curves of his calves, to the bent knees, down the smooth slopes of his thighs. He lingered on the rosy column of flesh that curved out from Kit's crotch before sliding over the contours of Kit's abdomen and pectorals until his gaze ascended the column of Kit's neck and came to rest on Kit's face.

"Come here," Kit murmured and Romy went to him.

Romy knelt between Kit's thighs and crouched over him, bending down until his mouth touched Kit's. Kit's lips parted, and Romy ran his tongue along them and inside. As he took Kit's mouth in a deep, wet kiss, Romy squeezed a stream of lubricant down Kit's cock and the crack of his ass. Shifting his weight, Romy tilted his head to a different angle and resumed the kiss while stroking a finger along the path the lube had taken. He swallowed a string of moans as he took hold of Kit's cock and pumped it. Giving Kit some air, he kissed his way down Kit's neck and back up. Taking the sweet mouth again, Romy moved his hand down to fondle Kit's balls. Romy's cock got a little harder with each sound of pleasure that was muffled against his lips. Letting his hand slip lower, he circled Kit's hole with his fingertip. Kit's ass lifted off the mattress, seeking more contact, and Romy stepped up the pace.

Snatching up the bottle of lube, Romy poured more on his fingers and some on his dick for good measure. He ran a hand over Kit's chest, plucking at his nipples, as he toyed with Kit's hole with the other hand. The sight of Kit moving restlessly against the sheets and rising into his caresses excited Romy to a fever pitch. He was sure he'd never been this hard in his life, and his cock literally ached to bury itself in Kit.

Gently, but insistently, he nudged his fingertip against the resilient ring that grudgingly gave way. The noises Kit was making encouraged Romy to push harder and his finger sank into Kit to the first knuckle. Kit snapped his pelvis forward, twisting his hips, and taking in more of Romy's finger. Seeing this as a definite sign, Romy eased his finger all the way in as he bent to kiss Kit again. While he thrust his tongue lazily in Kit's mouth, he shunted his finger slowly in and out of Kit.

"Please," Kit whimpered into Romy's mouth. "Give it to me now."

Romy kissed Kit again before he eased his finger out. Rising onto his knees, he took hold of his cock and nuzzled the tip against Kit's crinkled, pink hole.

"Yes," Kit said breathlessly. "Fuck yes. Give it to me."

Romy shifted his weight forward and brought more pressure to bear. Tightening his grip on his shaft, he worked the tip in. The portal clamped down on the head of Romy's cock and he paused as he shivered at the powerful sensation. He ran his palms up Kit's body, rubbing the smooth skin of Kit's belly and chest, soothing him before taking hold of Kit's hard-on.

Kit reacted instantly, bracing his feet against the mattress and thrusting up into Romy's fist. Romy thrust at the same time, pushing his dick deeper into the tight heat that was so alluring. Kit twisted against the sheets, groaning deep in his chest as he was penetrated by degrees. Romy's chest heaved with the effort of holding himself back from plunging into the channel that hugged his dick with such intoxicating strength. And the way Kit was moving around didn't do anything to help Romy's self-control.

"Come on," Kit said in a strained whisper. "Come on and fuck me."

"There's nothing I'd rather do," Romy said in a voice that seemed to vibrate in Kit's groin.

Romy raised Kit's legs until Kit's calves rested on his shoulders. Unhurriedly, he pulled out of Kit and hesitated for a beat before pushing back in. The lube eased the action as Romy withdrew and advanced, mesmerized by the sight of Kit responding with such unselfconscious ardor. When the sheer wonder of the fact that he was fucking Kit abated a little, he recalled some of his technique.

Kit cried out and pumped his hips as Romy altered the slant of his stroke. "Again," he ordered breathlessly.

Romy obliged, rolling his hips as he drove his hard length into Kit at the same angle.

Kit gasped. "Oh, fuck, yeah!"

Romy wrapped his arm around Kit's thigh and rocked into him, his gaze locked on the point where his cock moved in and out. Kit made a mewling noise, and Romy looked up into Kit's eyes. Kit lifted his hips and Romy was reminded that he was holding Kit's dick. Romy moved his hand up and down, squeezing the hard column of flesh in a counterpoint to his pistoning cock.

The tension at Kit's core coiled tighter with each stroke until it reached the snapping point and released him into a blooming cloud of bliss that spread through his body like ink in water, filling every cell with warmth. His cock jerked in Romy's fist and spilled warm fluid over Romy's knuckles. Transported by the powerful climax, Kit continued to pump his hips, urging Romy to find his own release.

Romy raised his hand to his mouth and licked Kit's essence from his fingers as he filled Kit's passage in short, languid strokes. Taking Kit's left leg down from his shoulder, Romy pinned it to the mattress as he increased the tempo of his thrusts.

"Yes!" Kit cried out, bearing down on the hard length of flesh that filled him in such a satisfying way. "Fuck me!"

Romy drove into the flexing sheath, his teeth indenting his full lower lip, as the exquisite friction built to a level impossible to sustain and his release erupted from the end of his cock. With a hoarse cry, he let go, and a bolt of pleasure lit him up as he shuddered through an intense orgasm. Gasping for breath, he held on to Kit like a man hugging a tree in a hurricane.

"Whoa." Romy said as Kit relaxed his inner muscles.

"Good?" Kit asked.

"Give me a second before you make me answer questions. I'm still seeing stars."

"And that answers my question." Kit moaned when Romy shifted his weight. "Damn, it feels good having you inside me."

Romy jerked when Kit tightened up again, and then sighed as Kit eased up. "Man, I haven't come like that in… ever."

A drowsy but pleased smile curved Kit's lips.

"Just… give me a second," Romy said. "And I'll… let you get more comfortable."

"You know what I love? Besides your dick in me?"

Romy shook his head, dark hair swaying against his shoulders.

"It's never awkward with us."

Romy turned his head to kiss the inside of Kit's knee. His five-o'clock shadow prickled against Kit's skin and left behind a burning tingle that was echoed in Kit's groin. Despite his recent climax and state of exhaustion, Kit wanted to do it all over again.

"What's that look?" Romy asked as he met Kit's eyes.

"Come here." Kit held out his arms.

Romy pulled out and peeled off the condom. During the split second when he was beginning to wonder what to do with it, Kit took it from him, deftly knotted it, and tossed it into the trash basket across the room.

"Impressive," Romy said softly as he stretched out beside Kit and propped his head on his hand. He ran his free hand down Kit's body from his chest to his humid crotch. Palming Kit's cock and balls, he squeezed gently. "Was everything okay for you?"

Kit put his hand over Romy's, encouraging him to continue his fondling. "Okay? I just had the most intense sexual experience of my life, and you want to know if it was okay?" He ran a finger down the curve of Romy's dick. "I don't know. I guess. If you think the pyramids are okay. Or the northern lights. Or *The Rocky Horror Picture Show*."

"What's that?"

"*The Rocky Horror*—?"

"Yeah, what is it?" Romy interrupted.

"It's a movie, but it's so much more. I can't believe you haven't seen it. You must be the only English-speaking gay man who doesn't know about it."

"We'll have to watch it sometime." Romy glanced down. "You're getting hard again. Anything I can do to speed the process?"

"You're already on it." Kit wrapped his hand around Romy's shaft. "I was so scared the sex was going to be bad, but I shouldn't have worried."

Romy's breath caught as Kit's hand began to move, and there was no more conversation beyond the occasional, profane expression of approval. They fell asleep on the tangled bedding, each wearing a smile of utter content.

Romy woke with his head pillowed by the curve of Kit's back and his hand resting possessively on one of Kit's round ass cheeks. Carefully, he rose and went to the bathroom. He managed to bend his morning wood down far enough to take a piss and went to the sink to splash his face. After getting dressed, Romy wrote a long note and left it on the pillow next to Kit. He didn't want to wake his lover, but he couldn't leave without kissing him, so he risked it. Kit's lips were warm and soft against his, and he had the intense urge to climb back into the bed. With a sigh, he turned away and went to work.

CHAPTER
SIXTEEN

KIT WOKE, stretched like a cat, and got out of bed. Hearing the crinkle of paper, he glanced back and saw the note. He picked it up and read it on the way to the bathroom. When he set it down, he looked up at his reflection in the mirror.

"Check that goofy grin," he said. "Who's in love? You're in love, that's who."

He picked up the paper and read it again. He could hardly believe this was happening, that a relationship was progressing so well with no sign of icebergs on the horizon.

"Crap," Kit said under his breath as he heard his phone. He found it in the living room, but by that time he'd missed the call. When he saw the number, he was tempted to ignore it, but it was better to get it out of the way so he could spend the rest of the day reliving last night until Romy returned. "Just do it," he told himself and poked the touch screen. "What do you want?" he asked when the phone was answered.

A few minutes later, Kit hung up and set the phone down with more force than necessary. So much for a pleasant afternoon daydreaming about what he and Romy were going to do tonight. The meeting he'd just agreed to would effectively ruin the rest of the day; however, he was still operating on the premise that it was better to get it over with than dread it. Feeling the need for fortification, Kit went to the kitchen and ate too much. After a long shower, he dressed in jeans and a T-shirt and flipped through a catalog until the doorbell chimed.

Kit answered the door, and there he was, the man who had made him shiver simply by saying his name, the man who had taught him that sex was more than furtive hand jobs, the man he'd thought he'd love forever.

Brandis Young was just as handsome as he'd always been, with those slightly tilted green eyes and pointy canine teeth that made him look like a smug werewolf when he smiled.

"Thanks for seeing me," Brandis said as Kit showed him into the living room. "This is a nice place. Not at all what I imagined for you, though."

"I'd rather not chat. I'd like for you to say what you came here to say and then leave, never to return."

"I'm serious about wanting you back."

"I can see that. What I can't see is why. You're straight, or have you forgotten?"

"Come on. Cut me some slack. I'm not the only bisexual man who ever panicked and tried to go the straight route."

"No, you're not, but you're the only one who broke my heart. I don't want you back in my life, and I certainly don't want you in my bed."

"But we were so good together."

"The sex *was* amazing, but that's really all you have to offer me. I have a man who gives me great sex and so much more. What do I need with you?"

"Cold, Kissy, ice-cold. Why can't you forgive me for getting scared and running off and marrying the first girl I ran into?"

"Because you ran into her on multiple occasions while we were still living together."

"That was wrong, but you have to understand the doubts I was having."

"You're a dog. Just admit it. You want all the pussy *and* all the ass."

"I want a family, and I'm willing to work hard and be a success to support them. I deserve a reward for that, don't I?"

"And that reward would be me?"

"I don't know why you're so resistant to the idea. Your life wouldn't have to change at all, except you'd live in an even better apartment nearer my office. I can offer you a very substantial salary to do nothing more than be available when I call. Would you like to be a partner? Just say yes."

"So this is really a business transaction."

"I just want you to know that you'd be well taken of." Brandis smiled. "I remember how you like being taken care of."

"I wonder what your wife thinks about this arrangement. Or is it a secret?"

"Of course it's a secret. No one can know. But if Katrina finds out, it won't be a problem. Even if she was curious, she knows better than to interfere in my business."

"Okay. Let me put this in terms you'll understand," Kit said. "I have no vacancy that needs filling. There's no open position for you here."

"Let me show you pictures of the apartment I picked out for you."

"No. Get it through your head, Brand. You won't change my mind."

"Kissy…." Brandis changed his mind about what he was going to say. Getting up from his chair, he held out his hand. "Let's talk when you're feeling better."

Kit stood up. "I've said all I have to say to you. Let me show you out."

"Don't bother. I'll call you tomorrow."

"Don't bother."

Brandis smiled. "One of the things I've always loved about you is your fire," he said before he left.

Brandis wasn't at all discouraged as he walked out of Kit's apartment. This was just the second in a round of sales pitches he had planned. The opening salvo had been fired at Eliza's barbecue, and the next would come in a day or two when Kit's nerves had had a chance to settle. Brandis didn't doubt that his campaign would end the way he wanted it to. He knew Kit and knew what strategies to use. A cooling-off period followed by a thoughtful gesture of some sort was the way to go here. Brandis made a note to have a case of really good wine delivered to Kit in a couple of days. Meanwhile, he was free to concentrate on other business.

Romy's heart faltered as he saw Brandis Young coming out the door of Kit's building. He ducked behind a newsstand and Brandis walked right past without seeing him. Romy tried not to jump to conclusions, but self-doubt conjured a host of painful possibilities. After all, Kit had once been passionately in love with Brandis. Sometimes all it took was a breath to rekindle an old flame. Romy's gut clenched so violently that he doubled over, fighting for breath.

"No," Romy whispered. *Not without a fight.* Not this time. He wasn't going to stand silently by again while his world crumbled in front of his eyes. He loved Kit Britten, and he was going to hold on to him with all his strength. Unclenching his fists, Romy walked into the building.

"Sorry I'm early," Romy said when Kit opened his door.

Kit greeted him with a kiss and dragged him into the kitchen to taste the chili he was cooking. "What do you think?" Kit asked.

"It's good. Are we having it for dinner?"

"Don't be silly. It needs to simmer for at least twenty-four hours."

"Right. My mind must've wandered."

"You do look a little distracted. What's going on with you?"

Summoning his nerve, Romy said, "I saw Brandis Young leaving."

"He pestered me until I agreed to meet with him. He said there were things we needed to settle between us, and technically, he's right. We jointly own an apartment in Paris for one thing." Kit met Romy's eyes. "Do you really want to hear this?"

"If it affects us, I'd like to hear it."

"It's so much like a soap opera that I almost want to laugh. First of all, Brand went to my family before he talked to me, and my parents are on his side. Of course, they don't know what he really means when he says he's offering me a partnership."

"A partnership?"

"He's offering me a position in his corporation, which is one of the fastest growing in the state right now. It comes with a luxury apartment and a bunch of other stuff, including the title of partner, which I find ironic. What he's really offering me is the position of chief executive whore. He wants me available for sex at his convenience. He hasn't changed."

"I guess I'm glad he hasn't."

Kit frowned. "Why?"

"I don't want him to have a chance with you."

"He doesn't. I asked him what would happen if his wife found out about his plans, and he said it wouldn't be problem. He implied that she'd put up with it whether she liked it or not."

"Now that's true love."

"More like a merger. Her dad owns a chain of electronics stores. Brand has an exclusive deal with them to use and sell the products his company imports."

"I can see why your parents think it's a great opportunity for you."

"They're going to be so disappointed I turned the job down, but I—" Kit shook his head. "My family might be in love with Brand, but I'm not, and that's what counts."

"What about Paris?" Romy had to ask.

"We were college kids on our own for the first time far away from anyone who knew us. There was such a sense of freedom. We behaved as we pleased, like two people in love. If Brandis was really the person he was in Paris, I'd still be with him. But as soon as we came home, he went right back to following tradition. Apparently, to him, being successful is more important than being happy."

"Can't you be both?"

"I don't know, but I don't want you to worry about him. I'll always treasure the year we spent in France, but if I went back there, I'd want to go with you."

"I like it when you talk about your future and I'm in it." Romy slipped his arms around Kit's waist. He leaned back, his crotch pressed solidly against Kit's. "And I'm sorry if my insecurity is annoying."

"I've never noticed."

"Bullshit. You called me out for it on our first date."

"You did the same to me on our second date."

"Well then…. I guess we're even."

"And that's the way I like it. You know, we haven't really discussed these things yet, so I'm just going to tell you that I'm perfectly happy on the top or the bottom."

"I'm partial to switching like we did last night."

"Maybe we should hang a bell over the bed to ring when we want to change it up."

"Lunatic."

"I love that you have a pet name for me."

"The fact that you love the pet name Lunatic just proves what a lunatic you are."

Kit kissed Romy. "And of course, you mean that in a good way."

"Of course." Romy kissed Kit back.

"So, do you think you're ready for dinner with my folks?"

"As long as I'm not the main course. Why do you ask?"

"I think it's time for several reasons. For one thing, I want my parents to get used to seeing us together. I think it'll lessen the shock when I finally do come out to them."

"Whenever you decide to do it, you know I'll stand by you."

"I believe you will. How did I get so lucky?"

"Dead ants brought us together, remember?"

"Oh, yeah, that was it." Kit fussed with Romy's collar for a few seconds. "If you're okay with it, I'm going to call mom and tell her we'll be there at seven."

"That doesn't give me much time to get a bouquet and a gift basket."

Kit pretended to slap Romy. "Clown," he said.

"Lunatic."

Kit smiled as he put his phone to his ear. Romy mimed a need for the toilet by crossing his legs and left Kit to make his call.

CHAPTER

SEVENTEEN

"THIS IS where you grew up?" Romy asked as Kit pulled into the driveway of a three-story, two-wing mansion.

"Mostly."

"It's big."

"Yeah, I used to ride my bike through the halls on the second floor."

"I thought your sister's place was grand, but this is really high class."

"Did I already warn you that dinner conversation can get pretty ugly?"

"Was that the part where you referred to your father as a pompous bully?"

"So you *were* listening."

"I listen to everything you say."

"I love that about you." Kit pulled around the side and parked with several other vehicles. "Looks like Jules and Katherine are here," he said. "I don't know who the compact belongs to. Well, are you ready?" He looked over at Romy.

"Can I get a kiss for luck?"

Kit gave Romy a quick kiss. "Okay, let's go."

"I'm right behind you... where the view is very nice," Romy said as he followed Kit inside.

Kit laughed and did an exaggerated sashay all the way to the front door. The door opened as they reached it, and a middle-aged woman in a maid's uniform let them in. After Kit greeted her by name, she showed them to the dining room. Romy found this amusing, since presumably Kit knew where the dining room was.

"Sorry we're late," Kit said as he and Romy walked in.

"Don't worry about it," Mrs. Britten said as Kit came around to kiss her cheek. "Why don't you sit beside me, and your friend can sit across from you?"

"It's O'Keefe, isn't it?" Mr. Britten said. "Nice to see you again. How's business?"

"It's steady, sir," Romy said as he sat. "But I wouldn't mind if it was steadier."

Mr. Britten chuckled. "I know exactly what you mean. How's the overhead where you are?"

Mrs. Britten cleared her throat. "You promised you wouldn't talk business during dinner," she reminded her husband.

"Well, what are we men supposed to talk about, then?"

"At the least, you might let Kit's friend say hello to everyone else first."

"I've met Jules," Romy said. "Nice to see you again."

Two of Kit's other sisters, Katherine and Margot, introduced themselves and Romy told them it was a pleasure to meet them. The maid entered to clear the salad plates, and Mrs. Britten asked if Kit and Romy wanted salad. Neither wanted to hold up the meal, and declined. A few minutes later, the first course arrived and porcelain bowls of lobster chowder were set at each place.

"So what's your line of work, Mr. O'Keefe?" Mr. Britten asked.

"Please call me Romy, sir."

"Romy owns a garage," Kit said.

"Oh?" Mr. Britten looked interested. "Tell me, is it a family business, or did you strike out on your own, Romy?"

"I worked for the previous owner and saved enough to buy the business when he retired."

"Good for you!" Mr. Britten said. "I don't see a great deal of ambition in most young people these days."

"Dad," Jules said. "Not this speech again, please."

"I'm not allowed to express an opinion?" Mr. Britten looked around the table as if seeking support.

"Perhaps not in front of our guest," Mrs. Britten said, smiling politely at Romy.

"Just one more business question," Mr. Britten insisted. "Kit, have you decided to accept Brandis's offer?"

"I've decided not to."

"I hope you're joking. Why would you turn down an opportunity like this?"

"It's too complicated to explain."

"I'm a reasonably intelligent man," Mr. Britten said. "Why don't you try explaining it to me?"

"I meant that I can't explain it to *you*."

"I can't believe you'd slap Brandis in the face like this," Mr. Britten said. "He's doing you a favor, and you don't even have the common—"

"Why don't we ask Katherine how her auditions are going?" Mrs. Britten said loudly.

"I'm not auditioning anymore," Katherine said as she pushed her half-empty bowl away. "I've decided to go into costume design."

"That sounds lovely," Mrs. Britten said. "Now aren't you glad I insisted you learn to sew?"

"Wait? Are you giving up on being a dancer?" Jules asked her sister.

"I'm not sure yet, but I *am* sure that I need a job that pays the rent."

"Darling, you can always come home, you know that," Mrs. Britten said.

"Thanks, Mom, but I have one last shred of self-respect left." Katherine smiled. "And honestly, I like working in the wardrobe department. Right now, I'm just making sure the costumes are on the right hangers and in good repair, but it's a start. Someday I'll be a designer."

"That's the right attitude," Mr. Britten said. "How are things with you, Margot?"

Margot's spoon clattered against the side of her bowl as she looked up from between the curtains of her hair. "I'm fine," she said. "Everything's normal."

"Meaning you're still slaving for that jerk dentist and spending every evening alone—except for that psycho cat of yours," Jules said. "The guy takes advantage of you, you know."

"Doctor does not take advantage of me." Margot turned to look at her sister.

"He makes you work overtime all the time and doesn't even pay you for it. You pick up his dry cleaning. You pick up his kids when they get sick at school. You pick out presents for his wife. Yeesh, when are you going to grow a brain?"

"You don't know what you're talking about," Margot said.

"You've got a huge crush on a married man who's using it to control you, and you don't even get any—"

"Jules!" Mrs. Britten said. "That's quite enough."

"I'm just trying to help her out," Jules said, setting her spoon down with a thump. "If she's too stupid to see—"

"Margot is your sister," Mr. Britten said. "Don't speak about her like that."

"Did you forget we have a guest?" Mrs. Britten added.

"I'm sorry, Romy," Jules said.

"No apology necessary," Romy said. "I'm Kit's friend, and you're his family. I hope you won't treat me like a guest."

"I told you," Jules said to Katherine. "Charming, right?"

"Bad manners seem to be in the air tonight," Mrs. Britten said. "Don't talk about Kit's friend as though he isn't here." She turned to Romy "It isn't always like this."

"The hell it isn't," Jules said under her breath.

"It's just like home," Romy said. "Isn't every family like this?"

Mr. Britten chuckled. "Very true. Only among family can you be truly honest." He turned to Margot. "Have you met any men recently who interest you?" he asked.

"She's thirty, Dad. Not exactly a spinster yet," Katherine said.

"I'm not being critical," Mr. Britten said. "Would I like a grandson before I die? Yes. Does that make me a bad father?" He looked at Romy.

Romy glanced at Kit. "Isn't there a term in chess for when there's no good move you can make?"

Kit smiled at his lover. "Yeah, the classic Dinner with the Brittens Blunder."

"My son is amusing," Mr. Britten said. "But women don't want a clown for a husband. They want a strong man who'll take care of their children."

"Actually, Dad, we want both," Jules said.

"When you bring a fiancé to this table, you can have an opinion," Mr. Britten said.

Mrs. Britten gasped.

"Don't shush me," Mr. Britten said. "I've had enough of this attitude. We raised them well, so why can't our children simply do the right thing?"

"What's the right thing, Dad?" Kit said. He knew he should keep his mouth shut, but he'd had enough of this attitude, too.

"Obviously you don't know, since you're still a bachelor."

"I'm never going to marry a woman and give you grandchildren." Kit swallowed. "Because I'm gay, and I'm in love with Romy."

Mrs. Britten gasped. "Kit, is this true?" Her gaze went to Romy, who was in shock. "What have you done?" she asked shrilly, her voice rising in volume.

"Calm down," Mr. Britten said. "Let's not get emotional until we know all the facts."

"I'm gay and that's a fact," Kit said. "I know that doesn't make you happy, but there's nothing I can do about it."

"Nothing you can do about it?" Mrs. Britten exclaimed before a look from her husband silenced her.

"Are you certain you're a homosexual?" Mr. Britten asked.

"Yes, Dad, I'm sure," Kit said wearily.

"No need for that tone. I read, you know, and I understand that homosexuality isn't a choice."

"Thank you," Kit said. "I'm happy to hear you say that."

"Let me finish," Mr. Britten said. "I understand that you can't help having those urges, but I still expect you to be a real man, take a wife, and raise children with her. That's a choice. The right choice."

"I can't do that."

"Of course you can. I know at least two homosexuals who have grandchildren."

"I won't do it."

Mr. Britten looked at Romy. "Do you have anything to say?"

"Just that I love your son, and I'll take care of him, sir."

"You'll have to. He certainly can't take care of himself." Mr. Britten cleared his throat. "Kit, are you certain this is the life you want?"

"Yes, sir."

"Be very certain before you make this choice. You have a lot to lose."

"If I don't have Romy, I don't have anything."

"Very well, you've made your decision, then. You don't how much this hurts me, but I can't support the life you've chosen. Do whatever you want to with the credit cards, but they won't work after tomorrow morning. You can have two weeks to vacate the apartment. The car was a present, so you can keep it, along with anything else that was given to you outright. I'd appreciate it if you didn't try contacting us after you leave here, unless it's to tell me that you've changed your mind. I'd also appreciate it if you'd leave as soon as possible."

"No!" Mrs. Britten got to her feet. "You can't throw him out."

"He's not four, Margaret, he's twenty-four." Mr. Britten put his hands on the table and levered himself up. Taking the cane propped against his chair, he hobbled from the room.

Kit stood and stalked out with Romy right behind him.

Seeing that her husband's mind was made up, Kit's mother ran after her son to plead with him. "Please," she said when she caught up with him in the entry hall. "Would it be so hard to marry one of your female friends?"

"I don't want to marry someone I don't love," Kit said. "And I could never feel that way about a woman. I'm sorry." He looked down. "I didn't mean to make Dad so mad, but I am what I am, and I can't change it."

"His leg is really bothering him today, and you know how he is. He won't take the pills."

"Mom...." Kit changed his mind about what he'd been going to say. Instead, he leaned down to kiss her cheek. "I guess I won't be seeing you, unless we meet in secret." He moved his eyebrows rakishly up and down to make her smile.

"Stop it," she said, blinking away tears. Putting her arms around Kit, she hugged him tightly. "Call me on my cell phone," she said when she let him go. "I know how to use it now."

"I will."

Romy cleared his throat. "Mrs. Britten, I'm sorry I—"

"Don't apologize, please," Mrs. Britten said. "I want Kit to fall in love with a girl and raise a family, but I also want him to be happy. If he can't do both, I choose happiness for him. Even if I can't understand that happiness." She patted Romy's forearm. "If you love my son, please love him well."

"I will."

"Come on," Kit said. "Before I start crying like a baby."

"You want me to drive?" Romy asked as they walked to the car.

"Yeah, that'd be great, actually." Kit got in on the passenger side and slumped in the seat. "What a spectacular fuck-up."

"It was impressive," Romy said as he started the car. "Can I ask one little question?"

"Sure." Kit looked listlessly out the window as they pulled onto the street.

"Could you have given me just the slightest warning that you were going to out us?"

"It just jumped out of my mouth. I was as shocked as you were."

"I don't see how." Romy braked at a stop sign. "Left or right?"

"Left and then straight through the light and you'll see the freeway signs." Kit leaned his head against the window. "I'm sorry," he said. "I shouldn't have done that."

"Well, it's done, and I did say I'd stand by you." Romy turned on the wipers as it began to sprinkle. "What do you want to do now?"

"You mean what do I want to do right now, or what do I want to do with my future since I obviously can't be a real man?"

"Both, though you seem pretty real to me."

"I swear to God, I don't know."

"Since we didn't make it to the main course, would you like something to eat?"

"I'm not hungry."

"Do you want to watch me eat?"

"I don't care. If you're hungry, let's get some food."

An exit came up as Kit finished speaking, and Romy cranked the wheel hard to the right. Romy downshifted rapidly as he swerved around a semitruck and sailed onto an access road that served several gas stations and fast-food restaurants. He ordered at a drive-up window and dropped the grease-spotted paper bag between his seat and Kit's. They'd gone less than a mile from the restaurant before Kit had to have a french fry.

"That smell is just not fair," Kit said. "I don't know what they put in the grease, but it's irresistible." He ate another fry as Romy devoured a cheeseburger in a few bites.

"They should make a perfume that smells like that," Romy said after taking a drink of his soda.

"Bad idea. The smell makes you hungry, not horny."

"What's your point?" Romy said as he stopped at a traffic light. "You feeling any better?"

"No, but at least we're together." Kit took out his phone. "I should let Ash know the cat's out of the bag. We had a kind of bet."

"A bet?"

"No, not really. It was more of an agreement about coming out, and I violated it. No big deal."

"All right. Do you want to go to your place? My place? Some other place?"

"My place, please." Kit put the phone to his ear. "Yeah, it's me," he said. "Guess who just told his mommy and daddy he's an ag-fay?" Kit paused. "Yes, I *did*. No, really. I did." He listened for a few seconds. "I didn't plan it. I just blurted it out. What?" Kit looked over at Romy. "No, he's okay with it. He was there, in fact, and he hasn't tossed me out on the side of the road, so yeah, I think he's okay with it. What?" Kit smiled. "We have to, do we? Well, then I guess we have no choice. Yeah, we'll see you there. Bye."

"Where are we going?" Romy asked.

"Ash's throwing together a Coming Out Ball for me. Want to invite anyone?"

"All my friends are on stage right now, and I doubt it's the kind of party I could bring Cardo to. At least, I *hope* it's the kind of party I can't bring Cardo to."

"I foresee rampant debauchery in your future."

"Will I be debauching with you?"

"I hope so. I need to really let go."

"Then I'm definitely not letting you out of my sight tonight."

"Good."

Kit reached over and took Romy's hand and held it until Romy needed to shift. He felt as though he'd been set adrift. His little life was about to get complicated, and he was certain of only one thing. Though he might lose all his money, his friends, and even his family, Romy was worth it. Kit just hoped he had the grit to live with his decision.

CHAPTER
EIGHTEEN

"MY GOD, how much alcohol did I drink last night?" Kit asked as he peered into his bathroom mirror.

"All of it, I think," Romy answered from the shower. "Why don't you get in here with me? You'll feel better."

"No way. If I get in there, I'm going to want to do things to you, and I'm too hungover to do them."

"I've never heard a better reason for cutting down on your drinking."

"Amen." Kit filled a glass with water and took a couple of tablets. "You don't have to work today, do you?"

"I could, but I don't have to." Romy turned off the water and reached out for a towel. "What do you want to do?"

"I want to move."

"Today?"

"I don't want to stay here a second longer than I have to."

"Are you sure that isn't the hangover talking? Why don't we go out for breakfast? You'll feel a lot better with something in your stomach."

"Are you asking to get puked on?"

Romy finished drying off, wrapped the towel around his waist, and wrapped his arms around Kit from behind. "Not one of my kinks," he said before kissing Kit's neck. "If you want to move, I'll help you."

"Thanks for standing by me."

"There's nowhere else I'd rather be." Romy hugged Kit tightly.

"I hope you still feel that way after we carry all my shit out of here. I can't afford to hire movers now."

"We'll get it done." Romy kissed Kit's nape and continued across the smooth skin of his shoulder. "I'm going to get dressed and see what's in your kitchen."

"Do you have to get dressed? The sight of you in nothing but a towel is cheering me up."

Romy shook his head. "Once a lunatic, always a lunatic," he said as he left the bathroom.

Kit looked into the mirror again and chastised his doppelganger. "Okay, so your head hurts, every cell in your body aches, and you want to sit in the corner and cry for a few years. Well, that's just too fuckin' bad, sunshine, because today is moving day. Now get your dumb ass in gear and get in the shower."

Romy was eating an omelet standing at the counter when Kit came into the kitchen. Kit paused to squeeze Romy's ass, which was irresistible in the jeans Romy had borrowed. They were Kit's slutty jeans, and they were quite snug, hugging the curves of Romy's muscular thighs and compact ass, and showing a lot of bare skin through the slashes.

"There's another omelet in the pan," Romy said as Kit poured a cup of coffee. "Nothing in it but cheese."

Kit shook his head. He was waiting for the pills to kick in and didn't want to impede them with food. "Thanks. I'll pass for now."

"It'll get rubbery."

"Let it. I support the right of all eggs to become rubber if they choose."

"Oh… kay. So where do you want to start with the packing?"

"First we need a buttload of boxes."

"No problem. We can scrounge the dumpsters behind the mall."

"Maybe I should organize some things first. Obviously, the furnishings belong with the apartment, but I do have a lot of personal stuff."

"Your clothes alone would fill a van."

"Yeah, I guess we need a van. The Ferrari isn't going to hold much."

Romy smiled. "I'm glad you're not brooding."

"Oh, I'm brooding. You just can't tell because of the hangover."

"Don't let it get you down, okay? Let's just keep moving forward until we're out of the rain."

"Are you trying to say that the sun'll come out tomorrow?" Kit sang the words.

Romy snickered. "Why don't you start organizing, and I'll call around and see if I can borrow a truck."

"Sounds like a plan." Kit took his coffee with him into his bedroom, made piles of his belongings, and started sorting them.

"How's it going?" Romy asked when he came in.

Kit looked around the room. "I'm being absolutely ruthless, but I still have too much stuff. We'll need a whole crew to move it."

"Then I take it you'd be glad to hear that a crew is on the way?"

"How did you manage that?"

"I knew Joplin and the boys would be waking up about now and that they'd be famished. I promised them brunch if they came over and packed. If we feed them pizza and beer later, they'll be happy to load your things in the truck."

"The truck?"

"My old boss called a guy who owed him a favor. The guy will be here sometime after five with a truck. All we need to do is tip him well."

"You think it'll be big enough?"

"It's got a twenty-foot bed."

"I love it when you talk dirty to me." Kit smiled. "So you did all this while I was puttering around in here?"

"It's been a couple of hours, babe."

"I must've zoned out." Kit glanced at his phone and noted the time. The Seconal he'd taken had smoothed things right out, and he'd had no sense of time passing. Nor had he thought about Brandis, the rift with his family, or much of anything at all for the past hour and forty minutes. "What about this brunch we're serving?"

"It's taken care of."

Kit started to ask for details but decided to just trust Romy. "Okay. Would you get the roll of bin liners from under the kitchen sink? We can stuff that pile of clothes by the chair in the bags and drop them at the salvage center."

For the next forty minutes, Kit and Romy worked together to get Kit's reduced wardrobe and other personal belongings into easily packed groupings. They bagged up the items of clothing Kit was giving away, and

Romy picked out a few things he liked. The bags were stacked against the wall in the entryway by the time brunch was delivered. Romy paid the deliveryman and carried the boxes into the kitchen. He and Kit had just finished setting out the deli food with plates and silverware when the doorman called up to say that Kit had several visitors.

"Come on in," Kit said as he opened his door. "Thank you all for doing this."

"Where's the food?" Koda asked, dropping his armload of flattened boxes on a bag of clothes.

"Good morning... afternoon," Joplin said, leaning the boxes he carried against the wall.

The Heater and Mark said hi and Kit led them to the table. After a few bites, the band members brightened, and soon Kit's apartment was filled with brotherly banter, raucous laughter, and random bursts of singing. When the food was gone, they assembled the boxes, took them into the bedroom, and filled them. The Heater was in charge of the packing tape, which they realized was a mistake after he taped Koda to a chair. Kit took over taping duty as Koda informed The Heater in some detail what he was going to do to him in retaliation. The Heater didn't look particularly distressed at these threats.

The crew moved into the living room and packed according to Kit's directions, before tackling the kitchen. Kit was taping the last box when Romy brought up a point.

"Where are we taking all this?" Romy asked. "Because it surely won't fit in the Airstream."

"I guess I thought I'd store it until I found a place. Wow, you must think I'm a real airhead. I've packed up all my shit, and I don't know where I'm going to put it."

"I don't think you're an airhead. I think you're under a lot of stress."

"Yeah, that must be it." Kit gave Romy a smile. "I need to make a call," he said.

"Okay. If the truck shows up, we'll start hauling stuff down."

"Thanks." Kit took his phone and went into his bedroom.

"You were stingy with details on the phone." Joplin turned to Romy as soon as Kit closed his bedroom door. "What's going on, Rome?"

"Last night, Kit told his parents he was gay. His old man owns this apartment, so he has to move."

"Harsh," Koda said.

"Yeah, it is," Joplin agreed. "But Kit had to know something like that might happen."

"I don't think he was thinking about that when he said it." Romy met Joplin's eyes. "I think he was just fed up with hiding who he is."

"So… he snapped?" The Heater asked eagerly. "Tell us more."

"There were some fireworks," Romy said. "Mostly from Kit's dad. That man is *not* a happy camper right now."

"Details." The Heater leaned on Koda's shoulder and looked eagerly at Romy.

"I'm not going to repeat what was said for your amusement."

"Well, excuse me for caring." The Heater tossed his head and pouted.

"Joplin," Romy said. "Tell me again how you ended up with a band that's completely gay."

"I put it in the ad." Joplin looked over as Kit's bedroom door opened. "Pop/rock show band seeks guitar player, must be gay. Pop/rock show band seeks bass player, must be gay. And so on."

"How did you know if they were gay or not when they auditioned?" Kit asked as he joined the group. "And don't tell me you have gaydar, because I don't believe in it."

"Neither do I," Joplin said. "I told them they had to sleep with me."

"We *did* sleep with you!" Koda exclaimed.

"That was of your own free will," Joplin said. "Not a requirement for joining the band. Last thing I need is a sexual harassment suit."

Kit chuckled as he turned to Romy. "If I may change the subject; Jackie, my realtor sister, found a storage place for me that's not far from the garage."

"I'm glad your dad's disownment or whatever doesn't extend to the rest of the family," Romy said.

"Me too. I probably won't get to see Mom much, though."

"Hey, who knows? Maybe she'll soften your dad up."

"I won't hold my breath. She actually agrees with him, you know." Kit paused when Romy's phone rang.

Romy spoke for a minute and put his phone away. "The truck is out front," he said. "Let's get moving. He can't stay parked there forever."

"I'll call down and see if Mr. Martinez can put out some cones," Kit said as everyone picked up a box. "Meet you at the elevator."

On the way down, there were several bad jokes about overloading the elevator and what would happen if they got stuck. Several cannibalism jokes were made, many with a sexual slant. They were still laughing as they marched through the door Mr. Martinez held open for them. The doorman told them not to worry about the truck being in a no-parking zone.

"Are you moving out, Mr. Britten?" Mr. Martinez asked.

"I'm afraid so," Kit said.

"I'll miss you, sir."

"Thank you, Mr. Martinez. I'll miss you, too."

When all the boxes were loaded, Romy's friends got in their van and Kit and Romy got in the Ferrari to lead the truck to the storage unit. It was getting dark by the time the truck was unloaded and drove away. Kit, Romy, and the band sat around on the boxes and caught their breath.

"I believe there was mention of pizza," Koda said.

"Restaurant or delivery?" Kit asked as he looked in his wallet. It was an odd feeling, having to check his funds, and the orderly rows of useless credit cards mocked him. He had a hundred or so in cash and a few thousand in his checking account, but he knew it wouldn't last long.

"We could go to the Brick," Romy said.

His suggestion was met with approval, and everyone drove a few blocks to a brick building with a beer sign in every window. Romy took Kit's elbow and held him back as the others walked into the lounge.

"This place isn't expensive at all," Romy said. "But they only take cash."

"I might need a loan. I don't want to cheap out and limit the number of pitchers."

"No problem. It won't come to much more than twenty dollars a head."

"That's not much for a day's labor. I should give them some cash too."

"Don't insult them. They're my friends and they like you. Leave it at that."

"I'll try." Kit slid into the big booth next to Koda.

"You'll try what?" Koda asked. "Whatever it is, I'd like to volunteer my body if it can be of service in any way."

"Smooth," The Heater said sarcastically from the other side of the table.

Romy sat down, thigh to thigh with Kit, and looked over at Koda. "I've got my eye on you, Romeo," he said.

"I hate being called Romeo," Koda said. "Dude had one hookup and died."

"I see you get my point," Romy said.

The Heater whistled. "Possessive much?" he asked.

"I just know what Koda's like," Romy answered. "He can't resist taking a run at anyone new."

Koda shrugged. "Everyone needs a hobby."

The waitress arrived, recommended a deal on a half-dozen pizzas and pitchers, and went away to place the order. Pitchers and mugs arrived and beer was poured.

"So where are you going to live now?" The Heater asked Kit halfway through his first beer.

"He's staying with me for as long as he wants to," Romy said.

"Okay, cool. I was just going to say he could room with me for a while. My couch folds out."

"As if I trust you any farther than Koda." Romy said as he refilled mugs.

"I'm hurt," The Heater said. "I made the offer out of the kindness of my heart."

"You should trust your friends more, Rome," Joplin said.

"I'd like to… but I know you so well." Romy laughed and raised an arm to fend off several flying straw wrappers.

Kit looked around the table. "Not to get too mushy or anything, but I want to thank you all for pitching in and getting it done the way you did. I'm not sure pizza is adequate payment for—Hey!" He broke off as he was pelted with straws.

"Shut up now," Romy advised.

"Was I saying something?" Kit asked innocently before taking a drink of his beer.

Six large pizzas and a lot of laughs later, they started talking about getting up from the table and leaving. Everyone knew they'd sit there until the beer was gone, but they talked about leaving anyway.

"Do you want to go back to your place or stay at mine?" Romy asked Kit.

"I can't think of any reason to go back there," Kit said. "I can have the clothes I'm donating picked up, and everything else is at the warehouse."

"You can really walk away just like that?"

"It takes a certain degree of bratty petulance you probably don't have in you."

"So this is a slap in your father's face?"

"Yeah, that's right." Kit finished his beer. "He gives me two weeks to vacate? Fuck that."

"So you're never going back there?"

"The maintenance people will water the plants. I can't think of any other reason to go back. Let them rent it out, for all I care."

Romy could feel the pain Kit was trying to mask with indifference. "Are you ready to go home to my place?" he asked.

"Yeah, just let me pay the bill. I've got it covered, but if you could leave a tip…."

"Got it," Romy said as he let Kit out of the booth to go to the register.

Kit, Romy, and the other young men said good night in the parking lot, and Kit and Romy went to spend their first night together as roommates.

NINETEEN

FOR A few days it was amusing to bang elbows, bump noggins, and collide whenever they turned around in the trailer, but Kit could see that the crowding was starting to wear on Romy, even if Romy never complained. Kit's feelings were hurt for about three seconds, and then he reminded himself that Romy was used to living alone in a space that was clearly designed for one. Kit told himself that he wasn't the problem and went to Romy to talk about it.

Romy slid out from under a station wagon when he heard Kit's footsteps on the concrete. "Hey, good-lookin'," he said brightly. "Time for lunch already?" He took the plate Kit held, went over to a couple of folding lawn chairs, and sat.

Kit sat down in the second chair. "I wanted to talk about something if you have time."

"Sure, what's up?" Romy bit into his sandwich.

"You're being really good about it, but I can tell it's driving you crazy having two people in the trailer."

"What?" A shred of lettuce fell out of Romy's mouth. "I love having you here."

"I know, but you have to admit that we could use a little more space."

"You really miss that walk-in closet, huh?"

"Well, I don't need *that* much room." Kit chuckled. "I was wondering how you'd feel about me looking for an apartment around here."

"I thought you were doing that already."

"So it's not a big deal?"

"No. Why would it be?"

"I just didn't want you to feel like I was looking down on living in a trailer, that's all."

"Babe, I don't think that you think you're better than me. Don't worry about it so much."

"I'm looking for a job, too. It wouldn't be fair to Eliza to go back to her shop. Dad would find a way to show his disapproval."

"It's only been a few days since the disaster," Romy said. "You're entitled to reel around in shock for a while."

Kit sighed. "Normally, I'd love to wallow in bed while someone—you—brings me treats and tells me everything will be all right, but I don't want to do that. I feel so restless. Like I just have to get out and do something… *anything*!"

"We could go out tonight, if you want."

"You've taken me out every night since my life blew up. We can't keep doing that. For one thing, we'll run out of money."

"Babe, life's too short to sweat the small stuff."

Kit gave Romy a curious look. "But you're always talking about saving money."

Romy put his plate down on the floor and came to kneel beside Kit's chair. Taking Kit's hands, he looked into his eyes. "I know we're struggling right now," he said. "Money's tight and we live in a matchbox. Sure, we need to worry about income, but once in a while, you have to give yourself permission to blow a few bucks on a good time. If you don't do that, your life will just be a grind, and by the time you feel like you have enough money, you'll be too worn down to enjoy it." He kissed Kit's fingers. "So stop stressing, okay? We'll be fine. We will. Just as long as we don't give up on each other."

Kit pulled Romy up into a hug. "I'm going to say it again. Thanks for standing by me."

"It's what people do when they love you."

"But really, we just started dating. You thought you were getting a boyfriend, not taking someone to raise."

"Shut up," Romy suggested as he covered Kit's mouth with his.

Kit parted his lips, inviting Romy's tongue to play. Romy straddled Kit's lap, leaning into the kiss, letting Kit feel how much he wanted him. Not averse to a little afternoon delight, Kit reached down to squeeze Romy's crotch. Romy leaned harder and the lawn chair collapsed in a tangle of bent aluminum. Laughing like children, Kit and Romy flailed around in a not too serious attempt to extricate themselves from the wreckage. Several more kisses and some roughhouse fondling later, they got to their feet.

"Let's finish this later," Romy said.

"Are you serious?"

Romy nodded. "I'm going to keep you turned on all day. By the time I make you come, you'll go off like a volcano."

"Oh my." Kit grinned. "In that case, I'm going to get on the phone and see what I can accomplish before you decide to tune me up again."

"Thanks for lunch."

"My pleasure." Kit smiled roguishly and went back to the Airstream to make his calls.

"Hey, Kissy," Jackie said when she answered her phone. "How are you?"

"I'm good, and I'm going to get better. How are you?"

"I'm glad to hear you're not sobbing in a corner with a bottle of barbiturates in your hand." She paused. "I'm so sorry. That was an unforgivably bitchy remark. I'm really glad you're doing well. I'm fine. Jennifer broke her arm playing soccer, but everyone else at home is fine."

"Is Jen okay?" Kit cringed at the thought of his thirteen-year-old tomboy niece forced into inactivity.

"She's fine. In fact, I'd swear she's proud of that cast."

"She's tough."

"I hoped she'd outgrow this stage by now."

"What if she never does?"

"Don't say that!"

"Why? She might grow up and be an Olympic athlete."

"I don't mind her being different. I just don't want her to be *too* different. Those are the kids who have such a hard time in school."

"Because ignorant kids *give* them a hard time."

"I've been putting my foot in my mouth all day. Did you need something?"

"Actually, yes I do. Thanks again for finding the warehouse. Do you think you could find a cheap apartment somewhere nearby?"

"Probably, but are you sure that's where you want to live?"

"This is where Romy lives."

"Okay, I get it. No need to elaborate. Let me have a look around, and I'll call you back, okay?"

"I really appreciate it. I know Dad would give you a hard time if he knew you were helping me."

"Well, he's wrong about this one, Kit, and I'm not going to side with him." Jackie paused. "Try not to be too hard on me and the other girls for not standing up to him."

"I understand, believe me."

"Thanks, Kissy."

"I love you, Jax."

"Love you, too. Bye now."

Before making another call, Kit poured a cup of coffee. As he was reaching up to get the sugar, Romy came in. Kit glanced over, saw the glint in Romy's eyes, and a shiver went through him. As he turned, Romy grabbed him and lifted him to sit on the tiny counter. Looking up into Kit's eyes, Romy didn't say a word as he yanked Kit's T-shirt up and nuzzled his nipples. Kit moaned, sinking his fingers into Romy's hair as Romy sucked and nibbled and switched back and forth without warning. Putting his hands on Romy's shoulders, Kit slid down until his crotch was pressed against Romy's. Abruptly, Romy drew back and pulled Kit's T-shirt down.

"You're evil," Kit said as Romy went to the door.

Romy gave Kit his best wicked smile and went back to work.

"He's going to drive me crazy," Kit said to the air. Sliding a hand under his shirt, he ran his forefinger around a wet nipple and savored the jolt of pleasure. "Yep, he's going to turn me into a lunatic for real."

Over the next three hours, several things happened on or around the premises of the garage. Jackie called with three apartments for Kit to look at. Kit made arrangements to see them that day. Romy ambushed his lover at intervals and stepped up the action until Kit was ready to scream. In fact, Kit did scream at least once.

"Aw," Romy said. "That's the first time you've called me asshole."

Kit licked his lips. "Come back here."

"No can do, babe. I have a part soaking in cleaning solution, and it's time to take it out." Romy blew Kit a kiss and hurried away.

Kit dropped back onto the bed and stared at the ceiling. The ceiling wasn't very far away. The "bedroom" was a space just large enough for the mattress with shelving built into the walls. It was a tight fit for two people and, even with judicious maneuvering, making love often involved the banging of heads on that ceiling.

After his most recent hard-on subsided, Kit told Romy he was going out, got in his car, and drove by the properties Jackie had found. He looked them over from the outside, took pictures with his phone, and went back to the garage. Romy molested him in the car, and then Kit showed him the pictures.

"They all look pretty much the same," Romy said. "Just pick the one you like best."

"You don't want to see them first?"

"Why?"

"I don't know. I guess I thought you might be interested in helping pick out the place where you'll be living." Kit paused when Romy's expression changed. "You *are* moving with me, right?"

"Of course. I was just waiting for an invitation."

"Really? Because you looked a little... horrified."

"Nope."

"Be honest please. I know you've lived alone for a while. I know how you can get into a routine that's comfortable. I know how nice it is to have everything right where you want it."

"And you're still inviting me to move in to your place?"

"You wouldn't be moving into my place. We'd be moving into our place."

"Then let's go look at apartments."

They looked at all three and decided that the first one met the requirements of being close to the garage and not having any bullet holes in the walls.

"You'd think they'd spackle over those and repaint," Romy said as they looked over the first apartment for the second time.

"What's that?" Kit called from the bathroom.

"The bullet holes in that last place."

"Stop exaggerating. You know those weren't bullet holes." Kit came into the bedroom and looked down. "Okay, I can live without a tub for a while, but this carpet...."

"Smells like stale french-fry grease and wet cigarette ash." Romy sniffed again. "And beer vomit."

"Gag," Kit said succinctly.

"Okay, we can rip this up and replace it ourselves. Joplin's brother will sell us carpet at cost. We'll need some furniture, mainly a bed, but we've got dishes and kitchen stuff." Romy looked around. "We can do this, right?" He turned to Kit. "It's not too small, is it?"

"We have a living room, a kitchen, a bedroom, and a bathroom. What else do we need?"

"Curtains." Romy nodded toward the windows that looked out on the windows of the building next door.

Kit snickered. "What? Are you too shy to give the neighbors a free show?"

"Let's give them one right now," Romy said as he pinned Kit to the wall beside the window and kissed him.

This time Kit was ready for the attack and turned the tables. Indulging his desire for this man who had taken him as he was, Kit held nothing back as he kissed and fondled Romy to an intense state of arousal. When Romy finally got a hand on Kit's crotch, Kit pushed him away.

"I deserved that," Romy said. "So, you want to go down and sign a rental agreement?"

"Let's wait 'til tomorrow and see if we still like it."

"Probably a good idea to sleep on it." Romy put an arm around Kit's neck. "Let's go home. I've got one more job to do, and then I'm taking you to dinner."

"Didn't we just talk about this? And if we're going to rent an apartment, we'll need every penny until I get a job."

"Come on. You can't say no to all the roasted corn and poblanos you can eat, plus a cold beer, and all for just five bucks."

"You're right. I can't say no to that."

"Tell you what. We'll get takeout, buy a six-pack, and eat at home in front of the TV."

"Outstanding." Kit hugged Romy. "When did we get a TV?"

"It's just an expression."

"What will we do for entertainment?"

"I'll think of something." Romy smirked. "I've kept you fairly well entertained today, haven't I?"

"I can't argue with that. Come on. Let's ask the guy to hold this place until tomorrow, and then we can swing by the tortilleria on the way home. I want a pound of shredded pork too."

"It's a while until dinnertime. How are you going to keep all that meat hot?"

"I've been doing fairly well today, haven't I?"

"Oh, that was bad," Romy said and chased Kit down the stairs.

"I'm going to have to think about those three flights of stairs," Kit said when they got to the ground floor. "They're going to seem like thirty if you're carrying anything heavy. And it's not like we'd have a view."

"That depends on the people who live across from us."

Kit talked to the building manager, and then he and Romy went home by way of the tortilleria. After carrying the food inside, Romy went back to work. Kit was daydreaming about living in the apartment with Romy when his phone rang.

"Hi, Ash," he said.

"I thought you were going to keep in better contact."

"If you called just to scold me…."

"I called for an update. I've been calling every day for a week."

"I've been kind of busy."

"Busy playing house with that dreamy mechanic?"

"You know his name. Use it."

"But I like the sound of dreamy mechanic much better. Anyway, where the hell are you?"

"I'm staying at Romy's right now, but we just looked at an apartment."

"That's wonderful! When's the housewarming party?"

"I hadn't thought about it yet."

"Well, start thinking about it right now! No, wait. I'll think about it for you. It's the least I can do when you're so busy being blissfully in love, you bitch."

"I love you, too. I'll text you the address, okay? Bye."

"You better," Ash said as Kit hung up.

Kit set out plates and rearranged the throw pillows on the couch. When it got dark, he lit some candles and reclined on the pile of cushions.

"You know what I was just thinking?" Kit said when Romy came in.

"No, what?" Romy asked as he shucked off his coveralls.

"The shower in the apartment is big enough for both of us."

"I like the way you think," Romy said as he pulled off his T-shirt. "Be right back."

"No, come here," Kit said, lounging back on the little couch that followed the curve of the trailer's nose.

"I'm pretty funky."

"Good." Kit worked a hand under his waistband and squeezed his cock. "Come share it with me."

Romy obliged, crouching over Kit and dipping his head for a long, wet kiss. Pushing a knee between Kit's thighs, he lowered himself until their crotches lined up and flexed his butt muscles, dragging his hard-on over Kit's. Kit braced a foot against the floor and lifted his pelvis to increase the friction while his fingers were busy removing Romy's ponytail holder. The thick waves of Romy's hair fell free to caress Kit's skin as Romy's kisses trailed down his neck and chest. Romy hooked a hand under Kit's thigh and raised Kit's left leg to rest on the back of the couch.

"God damn, that feels good," Kit said in a strained voice as Romy thrust again.

Romy grabbed the hem of Kit's T-shirt and pulled it up over Kit's head, baring Kit's torso. "Fuck, you're gorgeous," he said as he lowered his head again to lick, suck, and nibble at the smooth skin.

Kit grabbed a double handful of Romy's ass and squeezed as Romy pulsed his hips creating more of that delicious friction. He forgot about everything but the sight, smell, and feel of the man who was moving with him in such sublime harmony.

"That's enough for now," Romy said as he climbed off Kit. "I wouldn't want you to lose your appetite."

"Evil, evil man!" Kit bounced up. "You'd better run," he said as Romy disappeared into the miniscule bathroom cubicle.

When Romy returned, he hooked his MP3 player up to the speakers, and he and Kit ate a leisurely meal between bouts of foreplay. The teasing ended when Kit yanked Romy's briefs down and went down on him. Romy managed to maneuver himself around until he could get his mouth on Kit's cock. Both were primed to explode, but neither wanted to come first and each did his best to drive the other over the edge.

"Oh, my effin' God," Kit mumbled around a mouthful of Romy's balls.

Romy added more spit and eased his finger a little farther into Kit's hole. Not to be outdone, Kit pulled Romy's cheeks apart and reciprocated. Romy found the springy bump on the front wall of Kit's passage and rubbed it hard. Kit came in Romy's mouth, his cry of release muffled in Romy's crack. Pumping Romy's cock with his fist, Kit stabbed his tongue into Romy's hole. Romy came with a bone-deep shudder and Kit's dick slid from his mouth.

"Wow," Kit breathed.

"I told you it would be good," Romy said as he rested his cheek on Kit's inner thigh.

"Yeah, yeah." Kit took a moment to catch his breath. "It was really good. It was fantastic."

Romy wiggled around until he was face to face with Kit on the rug. "I'm surprised the candles survived," he said, before he kissed Kit.

"They knew this place was already on fire," Kit said sleepily.

"Hey, are you fading on me?" Romy asked.

"You wore me out."

Romy put his shoulders against the couch and pulled Kit to rest against his chest. Putting his arms loosely around Kit, he kissed the top of his head.

"This is really nice," Kit mumbled into Romy's collarbone.

"Yes, it is," Romy agreed.

TWENTY

IT TOOK a week—with the help of friends—to move Kit's belongings out of storage and find some new furniture for the apartment. Not that the furniture was actually new or that there was much of it. Kit picked up a fold-out sofa and two mismatched armchairs at a street sale and found a dining table with three chairs for sale at a local church thrift shop. He was being thrifty, but still his bank account dwindled, and he hadn't found a job yet. Though Romy never nagged Kit about it, Kit's guilt grew daily. One day, after Romy left for the garage, Kit called his mother.

"Is that really you?" she asked when she answered.

"Yeah, Mom. I'm sorry I haven't called you, but it just never seemed like the right moment."

"Well, I'm glad you did call. I've been worried about you, even though your sisters keep me posted. It makes me feel better to know you're not living in the street."

"Mom, don't be ridiculous."

"I'm sorry, but I worry. Do you need money?"

"Who doesn't? But it's okay, I still have some savings, and I'll find a job."

"I could send you some cash through Jules."

"Don't embarrass me. If I get desperate, I promise I'll call you."

"Promise?"

"Yes, Mom, I promise."

"It's not an easy world, is it, son?"

"No, it's not easy, but neither am I."

"Oh, it's good to hear your voice. I've tried talking to your father, but he's being stubborn. I'm hoping he'll be less grumpy after his steroid injection tomorrow morning."

"How's his leg?"

"He's in a lot of pain, dear. He won't say so, but I can tell."

Kit sighed. He didn't want to feel sorry for his father, but he did. "Is he taking his colchicine?"

"Yes, but he still refuses to take the pain pills."

"Why does he have to be so…?"

"Hush. Be respectful when you talk about your father."

"Yes, ma'am. I miss him, too."

"Because you love him."

"Yeah." Kit sighed. "I just wish he loved me back."

"Of course he loves you. You're his only son."

"I'm his *gay* son."

"Give him some more time, Kit. This is hard for him."

Kit wanted to ask if she thought it was easy for him, but he held the words in. She was caught between her husband and her son. No need to make things harder for her. "Don't let him drink," he said. "I'd better go. Love you, Mom."

"I love you, too."

Kit's phone rang as soon as he hung up. "Hi, Ash," he said, shaking off the somber mood that wanted to settle on him. "Is everything ready?"

"It's a go. Are you at home?"

"I'm standing by awaiting orders."

"I'll be there soon. I'm just leaving Trader Joe's. Should I bring lunch?"

"Bring some kind of food. I haven't been grocery shopping for days."

"I've got it covered. See you soon."

Ash arrived a half hour later, and Kit went down to help carry packages upstairs. Unloading required several trips, and the boxes and bags took up a fair amount of space in the living room.

"So what have we here?" Kit asked.

"Liquor, food, and decorations."

"Amazing. I have to say I'm impressed with Ash's Party in a Box so far."

"You haven't seen anything yet. Wait until I get it assembled."

"Should I get some batteries?"

"No, I brought those too. Which reminds me." Ash picked a gift bag out of the pile and handed it to Kit. "For you. A little housewarming gift I wanted to give you in private."

Kit pulled out the bright pink tissue paper and looked in the bag. "You're very naughty," he said as he took out a vibrator shaped like a fairly realistic, if anorexic, penis. "And I don't need it."

"There's lube in there too. Some rather intriguing flavors, if I say so myself."

"That I can actually use. Thank you." Kit hugged Ash.

"Did you look in the bottom?"

Kit pulled out an envelope. "What's this?" he asked suspiciously.

"It's not just from me. It's also from Eliza and a few other people. And yes, it's money."

Kit swallowed the proud words that came to his tongue. "Thank you," he said. "Please thank everyone else, too."

"When they heard about the housewarming, everyone wanted to send a gift."

"And *someone* suggested donations would make a lovely present?"

"Just accept that there are people in the world who love you, okay? Now let's get some glitter all up in this place."

Ash began opening boxes and handing items to Kit. "I know crepe paper is too cheesy for words, but look, this has glitter on it!" he said. "I figure we can just throw it around like this amazing rainbow tinsel I found." He tossed a bag to Kit. "Start blowing," he said.

Kit took out the multicolored balloons and did as he was told, while Ash chattered about his love life and the friends Kit hadn't seen for a while. By the time Kit was finished blowing up all the balloons, Ash had transformed the living room into a replica of a disco-themed junior high prom as imagined by a drag-queen diva.

"It sure is… sparkly," Kit said.

"Thanks." Ash began tying balloons to streamers. "So how's your love life? Besides more fabulous than Dolly Parton."

"The love part is great. The sex is beyond amazing. But we've had a couple of things come up."

"Did you fix them?"

"Actually, yeah we did. We confront stuff when it comes up and talk it out. It usually turns out we don't actually have a problem, just a misunderstanding."

"Glad to hear it. It's never good to bottle things up."

"Speaking of bottles...."

"Ready for a cocktail?"

"Absolutely." Kit led the way into the kitchen. "Hey," he said casually, "got any goof?"

"Not on me. I've got some Tuinal at home I can bring you." Ash opened a jar of jalapeno-stuffed olives. "If you think that's a good idea."

Kit set down the vodka bottle, abruptly afraid he was going to drop it. When his hand stopped shaking, he answered "No. I don't even know why I asked."

"That's why it's called a drug *habit*. Be a shame to waste that time you spent in rehab."

"I took a couple after Dad kicked me out." Kit confessed. He shook his head. "Who am I kidding? I had six stashed away, and I took all of them. I don't think it's a good idea to get more." He paused. "The fact I hid them from Romy should tell me something."

"Then you won't get any from me, so don't ask again, okay?"

"I won't." Kit took the olives from Ash. "So who'd you invite to the party?"

"The usual suspects, and Romy invited some people. He put together a party mix, too. Your man has good taste in music."

"Sounds like you two have been spending some time together. Funny, he didn't mention it."

"I asked him not to. There are a few surprises in store for you this evening. The money was just the beginning."

"Oh God, no!"

"Just go with it. You know I wouldn't do anything too outrageous."

"I'm doomed," Kit said as he hugged Ash. "Hey, listen, thanks for doing all this."

"I'm your best friend, remember? And besides, you need a good party right now." Ash hugged Kit back and let him go.

"That's the truth. You don't know anyone who'd hire me, do you?"

"I keep telling you if you'd just let me pimp you out, you'd be a zillionaire by Christmas."

"Ha ha, but I'm serious."

"If I hear of something I think would suit you, I'll let you know. Now finish making those drinks and let's get some hors d'oeuvres going while we have lunch. I'm hungry!"

Ash started pulling disposable serving trays out of bags and removing the wrappings while Kit mixed a couple of drinks. "Thank you," he said as he accepted a martini in a water glass. "By the way, there's a couple of boxes of plastic wine, martini, and margarita glasses around here somewhere. My goal is to have no washing up to do."

"A worthy aspiration." Kit took a drink of his supersized martini. "So what do you think of the place?

"I thought you'd never offer me the tour." Ash picked up his drink. "Let's go."

It didn't take long to see all three rooms, but Ash was full of compliments on how Kit and Romy had furnished the apartment.

"I love all the whimsical touches," Ash said. "You don't often see a tire-rim chandelier."

"Romy made that," Kit said. "Isn't it too deliciously kitschy?"

"It's even, dare I say, ironic."

"I have to make an effort to see more of you," Kit said. "You always *get* me."

"I think that tends to happen when you know someone from birth." Ash put a hand on the back of Kit's neck and drew him into a one-armed hug. "I love you, you know."

"I love you too." Kit returned the hug. "It's funny, but I swear I've heard those words more often since Dad kicked me out than I have in my whole life."

"Surely not."

"Okay, I'm exaggerating, but it's really encouraging to find out that I'm loved by such great people."

"Silly rabbit," Ash said fondly, and then looked up when someone knocked on the door. "Shit, they're early," he said.

"Is it okay if I answer the door?"

"Yeah, of course, I just thought I'd have time to mix up some frozen margaritas before the guests started arriving."

"Well, why don't you go to the kitchen and do that very thing while I see who it is?" Kit went to the door and opened it.

"'Scuse me, bro," Koda said, stepping around Kit. "Where's the kitchen?"

"This way," Ash called out and Koda followed the sound of his voice.

The Heater and Zippy came in behind Koda, each burdened with large cardboard boxes. Ash came out of the kitchen and began directing traffic, snapping out orders and using his hands like an orchestra conductor. No one disputed his rule as they began unpacking boxes. Joplin arrived and stood in the open door watching for a few minutes.

"Hey!" Joplin said loudly. "There's a lot more stuff in the van that needs to be carried up."

Everyone in the room looked to Ash.

"Well, go on," Ash said. "I'll organize a few things until you get back."

For a while, an ant trail bustled up and down the stairs transporting instrument cases and yet more alcohol from the van to the apartment. The musicians set up their equipment in a corner of the living room, thereby taking up half the space, even with the couch and chairs shoved against the wall.

"Maybe I'm getting old," Kit said. "But I'm happy to see you guys are going acoustic tonight."

"We didn't want to get you thrown out." Koda slapped Kit's shoulder.

"Right." The Heater looked up from the twelve-string guitar he was tuning. "We want you to stick around."

"Purely for selfish reasons." Joplin grinned at Kit. "When you're around, Romy's a lot more fun."

"Yeah, we've probably seen him more in the last month than all of last year," Koda said.

"I can't take all the credit," Kit said.

"Well, it's obvious to me that my boy Romy is head-over-heels for you," Joplin said.

"I'm crazy about him, too."

"You sound like a bunch of girls," Ash said as he came up. "Please continue."

Joplin cleared his throat. "I was just about to tell Kit that we're all sorry about his dad turning his back on him and that he has family with us if he wants it."

"Kit Britten hanging out with rockers," Ash said. "This makes me so happy in a way I could never put into words."

"Try," Koda said.

"Well, you know…." Ash looked flustered. "Since Kit isn't looking for anyone, I can feel free to…."

"Yes?" Koda leaned closer to Ash.

"Do a little poaching," Ash said quickly.

Koda crossed his muscular arms over his broad chest. "A poacher, huh?" He looked over his shoulder at his bandmates. "What do we do with poachers, guys?"

"Does someone need a spanking?" The Heater asked.

Ash's smile was bright with wicked glee. "Oh, we're going to be such good friends!"

"What have I unleashed on the world?" Kit said just as someone knocked on the door, starting a steady trickle of arriving guests. A half hour went by with no sign of Romy.

"Excuse me," Kit said to his friends. "I need to make a phone call."

"Has it been an hour already since you talked to Romy?" Ash asked archly and got a round of laughter. "Hey, Kissy," he called as Kit walked away. "Take whatever's in the oven out of it."

Kit waved and kept walking toward the kitchen as he took out his phone. *Where in the hell is Romy? And why isn't he answering his phone or texts?* When Romy's phone went to voice mail once again, Kit hung up in exasperation without leaving a message.

Kit had just taken the spinach dip out of the oven when the front door opened. Setting the casserole dish on the stove, Kit flung off his oven mitts and hurried to see who'd arrived. He was swept up in a wholehearted embrace that squeezed the air from his lungs.

"Am I late?" Romy asked.

"You were in danger of being the late Jerome O'Keefe, but I don't feel like killing you now that you're here."

"Sorry, but I had to pick up your present."

"It's not an ass-shaped cake, is it? Because there's already one of those on the dining table."

"See for yourself." Romy held out a small rectangular box wrapped in gold foil paper with a bright red bow.

Kit tore off the paper, which Romy caught before it hit the floor. As Kit opened the box, he smiled in delight. "It's exactly the same color as the Ferrari!" He took out the phone case and held it up. "I love it!"

"I know it's not exactly a traditional housewarming present, but I thought you'd like it."

"I *love* it!"

Romy kissed Kit and was reminded that they weren't alone when several guests advised them to get a room. "I'm in another world when I'm with you," he murmured to Kit as he let him go.

"A world without howler monkeys," Kit said loudly as he threw a dark look at their friends.

"Oh, quit bitching before we start hurling feces at you," Ash said. "Come and dance to this wonderful music."

Romy and Kit joined the press of bodies taking full advantage of whatever range of motion they were allowed. ImproVice had an impressive and eclectic stockpile of songs, and they sounded just as good unplugged as they did with speakers. There was no boundary between the audience and the performers, and Joplin did half his singing while dancing in the middle of the small crowd. A highlight of the evening was the pogo dance inspired by Joplin's bouncing to ImproVice's reggae version of "In the Navy." Another was Ash's slurred but heartfelt toast to the happy couple. And of course, the evening-ending attempt by Koda to reenact a scene from *American Pie* with the cake.

"That was historical," Romy said when the last two guests left around three in the morning. "We just threw *our* first party in *our* apartment."

Kit came up behind Romy and wrapped his arms around him as he rested his cheek against Romy's back. "Historical," he murmured. He was pretty sure that Romy meant *historic,* but so what? "I'm going to remember it for a long time."

Romy turned in the circle of Kit's arms and enfolded him. "Did you have a good time?"

"It was wonderful." Kit held Romy a little tighter. "We have a place to live. We have good friends. We have each other."

"Making a list?"

"Counting blessings." Kit kissed the side of Romy's neck. "I really think this is going to work."

"You know, you're the first man I've ever been serious about."

"Is that right?" Kit kissed Romy's Adam's apple.

"Not that I didn't want a relationship with someone." Romy tilted his head back as he shifted his weight from foot to foot. "But I have a real knack for picking up cheaters."

Kit swayed with Romy, dancing in place as his kisses spread farther afield. "I have no desire to cheat on you," he said between kisses.

"Someday you might run across somebody who tempts you."

"Doesn't mean I'll do anything about it." Kit left off unbuttoning Romy's shirt to look him in the eye. "You're all I need."

"Just promise me you'll tell me."

"You'll know when I'm planning to sleep with someone else because I will have left you. Now stop talking about stupid hypothetical situations and open your present."

"You got me something?" Romy took a step back as Kit reached into his pocket.

"Of course I got you something, but I had to torture you by letting you wonder all night. Plus, I didn't want to give it to you in front of everyone. Hold out your arm."

Romy watched Kit's fingers as Kit deftly fastened the plain silver cuff bracelet around his wrist. He held it up to admire it and saw the Armani logo.

"It's beautiful, but you shouldn't have spent so much on me."

"Relax, I didn't."

"Really?"

"Really. It's kind of a regift. I hope that isn't too tacky. It's never been out of the box until today, and when I remembered it, I knew it would look amazing on you."

Romy took another look at the polished silver gleaming against the dark skin of his forearm. "I like it," he said. "I don't wear much jewelry because of the job, but this is something I'd bother to put on after I wash up."

"High praise indeed." Kit laughed softly as he leaned in to kiss Romy.

"I'm exhausted, but I don't have to work tomorrow, so I have all night to show you how much I like my present," Romy said.

Kit felt the thrilling frisson of sensual excitement that ran through him whenever Romy looked at him that way. "I happen to have a brand new assortment of flavored lube," he said.

"I like the way you taste." Romy took Kit's mouth, pulling Kit into an embrace as their tongues got frisky.

They progressed from the kitchen through the living room to the bedroom in a series of sexual sojourns that had both on the edge of exploding. Dropping onto the bed in a tangle, they rolled until Romy was uppermost. He folded one of Kit's legs back and took hold of his cock.

"Shit," Romy said under his breath.

"What? What are you waiting for?"

"Forgot the rubber," Romy said.

"It's all right. You told me you're clean, and I trust you."

Kit came as Romy pushed into him and Romy came in a swift spate of thrusts. Bones melted by the hot rush of pleasure, they puddled together and were absorbed by sleep.

CHAPTER
TWENTY-ONE

"CAN YOU do me a favor?" Kit said as he came out of the bathroom wiping shaving cream from his face.

Romy looked up from his bowl of oatmeal. "Of course."

"The concierge where I used to live called and reminded me I had something in storage there. Could you pick it up for me? I'd go, but I have job interviews." Kit paused. "You know what? It isn't urgent, just a box of stuff I collected when I was a kid, as kids do. I can go this evening."

"I don't mind going."

"Are you sure? You can take my car."

"How are you going to get around?"

"I have a bus route planned out already. It's easier than driving would be."

"Okay, then. Any excuse to drive the Ferrari." Romy put on his denim jacket. "Do I look dashing?" he asked, holding up his wrist to show off his new bracelet.

"You look like a desperado. That was my first impression of you, if you're interested."

"A desperado, huh?"

"It's those dark, smoldering eyes. The first time you looked at me, I just about melted. I wanted you to throw me on your horse and take me to your hideout to have your way with me."

"Lunatic." Romy kissed Kit. "Good luck with your interviews," he said as he left the apartment.

Whistling happily, Romy got into the Ferrari and started it up. There were few finer things in life than a ride in a really nice car, and Romy thoroughly enjoyed the forty-minute drive to Kit's old apartment building. He parked in the structure across the street and walked out to the sidewalk. As he waited for traffic to stop, he had the peculiar sensation of déjà vu as he watched Brandis Young walk out of Kit's building. However, this time Romy didn't hide. Brandis was still standing under the awning when Romy arrived. Romy nodded at the other man and started to walk on by, but Brandis called out to him.

"Kit's not here."

Romy responded with flippant sarcasm, his default reaction to arrogance. "I know. He couldn't possibly be."

"Implying that you know where he is."

"Are we really going to have this conversation?"

"I think you're aching to have this conversation."

Romy clenched his jaw. "I'm not doing this on the street."

Brandis walked a few steps to the side of the building and looked back at Romy. "Is this enough privacy for you?" he asked, gesturing toward the gated service alley.

Romy's stomach roiled, but he wasn't going to back down from this. If Kit's ex needed a confrontation to get it through his head that Kit wasn't available, then Romy was going to let him have it. All Romy had to do was keep his head and keep his fists at his sides.

"Say what you need to say," Romy said as he stepped out of sight of the street.

"I just want you to know that I'm going to get Kit back."

"You've already made that clear, but I don't get it. Why do you even want Kit if you're supposed to be a big ol' heterosexual stud who spends all his time making money and trying to knock up his wife?"

"You know why I want him. He's... him. He's just so alive and when he enjoys something, he enjoys it with his whole body and soul. Have you ever seen him with a milkshake? It's downright erotic. Plus, he's mine and always will be."

"You say that with such confidence. Do you have him under some kind of magic spell or something?"

The corners of Brandis's mouth turned up. "The reason Kit will always love me is I was his first. He was a virgin before we got together." His smile broadened. "He was so sweet."

Romy stared steadily into Brandis's eyes but didn't reply.

"He was really eager to do it," Brandis went on. "He wanted to lose his cherry so badly. We were both minors, so why not? I showed him what to do and after that, he was mine." He shrugged. "And like I said, he always will be."

Romy held his tongue.

"You think he'll stay with you?" Brandis chuckled. "You're not in his class. Nowhere near it."

Romy was finally stung into replying. "And you think you're going to take him away with your money?" He snorted his derision. "You lived with him for two years, and you don't know him any better than that?"

"You're the one who doesn't know him. Kit needs to be taken care of, and sooner or later, a situation will arise that will send him running back to me. Because he knows I can take care of him like you never could."

"He seems happy where he is."

"For now. Why don't you keep supporting him for as long as you can? For as long as he can stand a Hamburger Helper diet with his lobster appetite. But one day, he's going to miss all the things I can give him, and he's going to leave you. It's just that simple."

"Look, I can see you want me to think Kit's using me, but I know that's not the case. Just accept that he's with me now, that we love each other, and we're going to spend the rest of our lives together."

"Really? Kit Britten living the rest of his life eating beans, drinking cheap beer, and shopping at discount stores? You're really naïve if you believe that."

"I'm not naïve. I just trust Kit. Something you probably had trouble doing. Something that no doubt led to him running away from you as fast as possible."

"Oh, good, you're going to try to get under my skin."

"I had you pegged for the kind of guy who loves to argue and loves to win. Why didn't you become a lawyer?"

"Good shot, but a swing and a miss. I happen to have a law degree."

"Ouch! I probably should have seen that one coming."

"Come on, O'Keefe. Give it up. You were beaten before you were born. You're outclassed and just plain out… manned."

"Wait, hold on. Are you saying you're more of a man than I am?"

"Isn't it obvious?" Brandis shook his head. "You're a fag."

"So you're superior to me because you sleep with women?"

"Again, isn't it obvious?"

"Does Kit know you feel this way about gay people?" Romy asked. "You're aware that Kit's gay, right?"

"What's your point?"

"I just don't see how you can square those two things."

"I want what I want," Brandis said.

"That's your answer?"

"And I get what I want."

"So I can consider myself warned? Is that it?"

"You can, but honestly, I never saw you as a threat."

"All that proves is how stupid you are." Romy clenched his hands. *Stop it. Can't let this escalate into a fight. That would only prove how stupid I am.* "I'm really enjoying our enlightening conversation and sparkling banter, but I have to pick something up and get home, so…." He turned toward the door of the apartment building.

"You think this is over because you're walking away? Believe me, it's just a matter of time before Kit is mine again."

I should keep walking. Romy turned to face Brandis again. "You keep saying that. Are you trying to convince me or yourself?" He lowered his voice. "Because deep down you know you're a loser who lost the best thing he ever had. Now, leave Kit alone."

"Or what will happen?" Brandis said, but Romy had turned toward the door again. "I'm curious," he called after Romy.

However, Romy had said his final word on the subject and had nothing else to say to Brandis Young. He went to the concierge's desk and asked for Kit's belongings. A rectangular box was brought to him; he signed for it and went back out into the day. The sun was bright after the cool gloom of the lobby, and Romy's eyes were dazzled for a moment.

"Hello, sir," the doorman said. "Do you remember me? Mr. Martinez?"

"Of course. Nice to see you."

"Do you ever see Mr. Britten?"

"Every day."

"Please tell him that he's missed. Such a nice, polite young man."

"I'll tell him, Mr. Martinez." Romy nodded and walked away. He was fine until he got to the car. As soon as he was alone, his stomach betrayed him. The very notion that he could lose Kit made him sick. He opened the car door and retched. After spitting a few times, he shut the door, and wiped his mouth with a take-out napkin. Tilting the rearview mirror down, he looked into the eyes of his reflection.

Stop it right now. Calm down and listen to your heart. You know Kit would never leave you for that guy. He just wouldn't. Trust him and trust your love.

Romy pushed the Ferrari's starter button and let the sound of the engine soothe him. The internal combustion engine was a wonderfully simple and logical thing, and if anything went wrong with it, Romy could fix it. After patting the dashboard like the head of a dog, Romy pulled into traffic and went to the garage. He put on the pair of coveralls he kept in a battered locker and did some work. When Kit called, Romy finished up and went home.

"HERE YOU go," Romy said, holding out the box as he walked into the apartment.

Kit put the box on the table and cut the tape that held the lid on. Inside were a couple of cigar boxes, some velvet bags that used to hold a popular brand of scotch, and several motley loose items. Kit slapped Romy's hand as Romy reached for one of the objects.

"Oops, sorry! That was a leftover reflex from the playground." Kit picked up the little metal car and handed it to Romy. "Actually, I want you to have this."

Romy studied the bright blue T-Top Corvette, lifting the tiny hood and inspecting the miniature tires and steering wheel. "This is beautiful," he said. "Almost pristine condition."

"That's the one I never played with. My dad put it away and didn't give it back until I got too old to play with model cars."

"There's a cut-off age?" Romy bugged his eyes.

"There was for me." Kit picked up something that looked like a plastic Swiss Army knife. "Man, I remember this."

"What is it?"

"I'll show you later." Kit stuck his hand in one of the bags with a look of great pleasure. "My polished rock collection," he said. "It feels amazing the way they slide around your hand." He handed the bag to Romy as he lifted out one of the cigar boxes. "These are trading cards, I'm pretty sure. Yep." He closed the box again and took out the other one. "And these would be ticket stubs, and brochures, and stuff like that."

"You liked keeping souvenirs when you were a kid, huh?"

"Yeah. I liked holding on to little pieces of the good times I had. I stopped doing it about the same time I started doing *it*."

"There's probably something Freudian in that, but damned if I know what." Romy tried to think of something to say to steer the conversation away from Kit's first sexual experience. "What's that?" was the best he could come up with, as he pointed at an object.

"This?" Kit picked up a round medallion on a length of wide ribbon. "This is my medal."

"An honest-to-God medal? Tell me, what did you have to do to earn something so prestigious?"

"I jumped into the water."

"You were a diver? That's interesting."

"Well, if you must know…."

"I must."

"I was a platform diver right up through eighth grade. I won a few medals, but this is the only first place one. The others are in a case at mom and dad's with all the girls' trophies."

"Lots of winners in your family, huh?"

"Losing wasn't exactly… acceptable. Dad demanded the best from us at all times." Kit set down the medallion. "I can't imagine how disappointed in me he is."

"Hey, you know what? It's okay." Romy put his arm around Kit and squeezed. "It's okay that he's disappointed. You don't have to live his idea of a life. It's the twenty-first century and your dad's not some Borgia dude building empires and arranging marriages. Live the life you want to live. Live the life that makes you happy." He kissed Kit on the temple.

"That's exactly what I needed to hear." Kit raised a hand to wipe at his eyes. "Looking at this old stuff has me all emotional. Is it absurd to pity the kid you were?"

"It's kind of pointless, but no, I don't think it's absurd. Were you unhappy a lot when you were a kid? You don't have to tell me, but I'm here if you need someone to listen to you."

"My childhood wasn't unhappy. In fact, it was pretty good. My parents and sisters spoiled me outrageously. We were always going on family trips to snow ski or scuba dive or something like that. Sure I had to study hard and practice hard, but most of the time it was cake, ice cream, and ponies."

"You had a pony? What am I saying? Of course you had a pony."

"Yeah, so I was hardly deprived. It wasn't until I realized that my fondness for other boys was a big no-no that I started being unhappy a lot of the time."

Romy shifted Kit around so he could hold him. "Yeah, that's a tough one," he said. "You grow up hearing and telling fag jokes without really understanding them, and then one day, you realize that you're a fag."

Kit nodded. "You're this horrible, disgusting, unnatural freak."

"Except you're not." Romy rubbed his cheek against Kit's. "You're just another human. The human I love, for what it's worth."

"It's priceless to me."

"You're making fun of me now, right?"

"Maybe a little." Kit smiled. "On the bright side, you cheered me up. Melancholy all gone."

"Good." Romy thought Kit had gone from downcast to normal awfully fast, but he was glad. "You feel like eating leftover lasagna?"

"Way ahead of you. It's in the oven, and I made a salad."

Romy picked up the little blue Corvette and looked it over again. "Thanks," he said. "It's a great model."

"The doors open, too."

"Cool." Romy opened both teeny doors and closed them again. "Where are the roof panels?"

"I told you my dad put this model away, right? Well, I found out where he kept it, and I used to sneak it out and play with it. One day, when I went to put it away, I couldn't find the roof panels. I put it back and prayed my dad never looked at it. From that day forward—" Kit paused dramatically. "I lived in fear."

"So your dad was right."

"Yes and no. He was right that I'd break the toy, but he should've remembered that to me, it *was* a toy, not some collectors' item. He should've bought his own Corvette if he wanted to keep it in the box."

"What happened when he found out that parts were missing?"

"He didn't, as far as I know. He just handed the box over after I put away my other cars. Maybe he looked inside, I don't know, but he never said a word about it." Kit shook his head.

"My old man never bought me one thing that was new." Romy shook his head. "You believe that? Every birthday and every Christmas, the presents were used. They all had dents, chipped paint, and other kids' names written on the bottom with Magic Marker. He always bought the presents, too. Mom had no say in it. I heard him tell her once that he couldn't trust her to buy the right kind of toys. He said she'd turn his sons into sissies if he let her."

"I guess he was right, too."

Romy looked startled for a second and then burst into laughter. "I was pouring out my heart," he said reproachfully.

Kit kissed Romy on each cheek and on the lips. "No more bad memories, okay? Let's go eat and have wild sex."

"At the same time?"

"Whatever you want."

It was quite a while later that Kit showed Romy the mysterious plastic gadget from his boyhood treasure box. Leaving the bedroom for the kitchen, he poured some dishwashing liquid into a saucer and carried it back with him. In the doorway, he paused to take in the sight of his lover sprawled on the bed, long limbs tangled in the sheets, sweat drying on his skin.

"What have you got there?" Romy asked in a sleep-rumbley voice.

Kit smiled impishly as he deployed the plastic toy, which held an array of bubble wands. Dipping one of the wands in the soap, he blew a stream of bubbles toward the bed. The bubbles drifted across the room to pop on the sheets and on Romy.

"That tickles." Romy lifted his head. "Come here."

Kit shook his head and blew more bubbles.

"Don't make me come get you."

Kit snickered and blew more bubbles.

"I'm getting up," Romy warned.

Kit retreated, blowing bubbles as Romy stalked toward him. "Okay. Okay," he said as he reached the couch. "I'm stopping."

Romy tackled Kit to the sofa amid much laughter and that's where they spent the night. Somehow, with all the reminiscing and hot sex, Romy forgot to mention that he'd seen Brandis. He wished he could forget Brandis entirely. Things were going really well with Kit, and Romy didn't need any old boyfriends hanging around making him nervous. When he was nervous, he made mistakes, and he didn't want to make mistakes where Kit was concerned. And he definitely didn't want his fear of losing Kit to be the thing that made Kit leave him.

CHAPTER

TWENTY-TWO

"SOMETIMES I really miss Mr. Martinez," Kit said as he finagled the stairwell door open while balancing two grocery bags.

"Who?" Romy said from behind Kit.

"You remember." Kit stood aside and kept the door from closing until Romy walked through. "The doorman at my old place."

"Oh yeah." Romy started up the stairs, shifting the box he carried to a better position. "I forgot to tell you he said hi. It went completely out of my mind after Young—" He stopped in midsentence and walked a little faster.

"*Brandis* Young? What about him?" Kit caught up on the second-floor landing.

"I saw him when I went to pick up that box for you last week," Romy said as casually as he could.

"And you never thought to mention it?"

"I don't tell you about every single person I see every day."

Kit heard the defensive tone and looked up from fitting the key into the door lock. "What happened?"

"Why do you think something happened?"

"Because you're avoiding the subject, which is unusual for you." Kit opened the apartment door and went inside to put the groceries on the counter. "Why are you so small?" he asked the kitchen.

"Are you going to say that every time we bring home groceries?"

"What?"

"About the kitchen being so small."

"Do I say that every time?"

"Well, three times so far."

"And it bothers you?" Kit waited but Romy didn't reply. "Babe, I'm not blaming you because the kitchen is small. I'm just making a joke about it. A feeble joke, as it turns out."

"It's just that I know you're used to way better, and I wish I could give it to you."

"Are you saying this because of something Brand said to you?" Kit brought the conversation back to the original subject.

"What difference does it make who said it, if it's the truth?"

"That's what you believe? That I'm doing you a favor by being here?"

"I saw how you lived before you met me. I wouldn't blame you if you missed all those nice things."

Kit's temper flared. "Do you have any idea how fucking insulting that is?"

"That wasn't my intention."

"So you didn't mean to say that I'm so shallow I'd choose money over you?"

"Speaking of money, how did the interviews go?"

Thrown off stride, Kit stammered. "They didn't.... I didn't.... None of the jobs were right for me."

"Did any of them pay actual money?"

"Yes, but—"

"But what?"

"Firstly, I don't want to come home smelling like a french fry every night. Secondly, no amount of money could make me work for a homophobe. And thirdly, I wasn't born to handle garbage."

"So you draw the line at getting dirty?"

"That's right, because I'm not a real man after all. I'm not a big, strong mechanic like you."

"Whoa. I didn't say that." Romy held up his hand like a cop stopping traffic.

"Are you shushing me?"

"No. You're taking my words wrong." Romy groaned in frustration. *How has this gone from grocery shopping to global war so quickly?* "Maybe I should just stop talking."

"Maybe you should, if all you're going to do is doubt me and yourself."

Romy turned away and went into the bathroom.

"Are you really through talking?" Kit called out. When Romy didn't answer, he took out his phone and punched in a number.

Romy heard the small beeps of the phone, and he froze with his hand on the cold-water tap.

"Hi," Kit said. "I need to talk to you, and I need you to listen, okay, Brand?"

At the sound of Brandis's name, an electric shock went through Romy's body. After a momentary struggle between curiosity and fear, good manners won out, and he shut the door. He turned on the shower, got undressed, and stepped under the hot spray.

"Stop talking and listen, or I'm hanging up." Kit paused, glancing toward the sound of the shower. "All right. I was hoping this wouldn't turn into a big, hairy drama, but you can't seem to get it through your head that you can't have me. So I'm telling you for the last time to stay away from me. Stay away from my family, and stay away from my friends. And most of all, stay away from Romy. If I find out you've fucked with him again, I'll make you sorry." Kit hung up and turned his phone off.

"Romy," Kit called out. "I'm going for a walk."

Romy heard Kit's voice, and nothing about the tone compelled him to get out of the shower. He shampooed his hair, lathered up everything else, and got back under the water to rinse off. He didn't want to think about what Kit had to say to Brandis, nor did he want to know where Kit was going right now. Actually, he was intensely curious, but he was afraid of what the answers might be.

Romy's phone rang as he was toweling his hair. It was Cardo's ringtone, so he picked it up even though he didn't particularly feel like talking right now.

"Bro!" Cardo said brightly. "What's the haps?"

"Did I just step into a time warp?"

"Are you dissin' me?"

"What's up?"

"I haven't seen you in a little while. Thought you might want to come over and hang while Mom's at her book-club thing."

"Aw, man, I'm not the best company right now."

"Why not?"

"None of your business."

"Bullshit. It directly affects me."

Romy draped the damp towel over the bar. "You have a point." He walked into the bedroom. "I kind of had a fight with Kit."

"What? Did zombies eat your brain?" Cardo made a disgusted noise. "Don't fuck this up, big brother."

"I'm not trying to."

"What did you fight about?"

"I'm not taking relationship advice from my fourteen-year-old brother."

"It's not like I could do much worse."

"Again, you have a point. All right. I'll tell you briefly. He got mad because I forgot to tell him that I ran into his ex."

"Ran into? Like with a car or something?"

"No, gorehound."

"But you did rip him a new one, right?"

"You don't even know this guy."

"He let Kit get away. He's either a jerk or an asshole."

"You're fourteen. Where do you get this stuff?"

"I'm right, aren't I?"

"The guy's a world class heavyweight champion asshole."

"Has he been bothering Kit?"

"Take it easy," Romy said. "No need to declare vendetta. Like I said, I talked to the guy."

"Why does that make Kit mad?"

"Thank you. That's what I said." Romy pulled a T-shirt on. "His reason is that he wants me to let him handle it because it's a problem from before he knew me."

"Okay, I can see that."

"Then it turned into an argument about money."

"I used to hate it when you and Mom talked about money. You were always so serious and worried looking. You aren't driving him crazy with your penny-pinching, are you?"

"I'm not a penny-pincher. Sure, I like to put away a little money every week, but I splurge once in a while."

"When?"

"I go to a club at least once a week."

"That's not splurging."

"It's splurging within my means."

"I think that's a contradiction in terms."

"When did you learn so many big words?"

"I have this big brother who beats me if I don't study, but Romy, seriously, make up with Kit. If you were wrong, just apologize. If you weren't, apologize anyway."

"And when did you get so cynical?"

"All I'm saying is: don't let your pride come between you and Kit."

"You should have a call-in radio show."

"You're hopeless. Smooth things out with Kit, and come on over. Both of you."

"We'll see. Meanwhile, maybe you should get off the phone and do some homework."

"Bye."

"See you."

Romy put his phone down, finished putting the groceries away, made a sandwich, and sat down in front of the secondhand television to wait for Kit. The ringing of his phone woke him three hours later.

"Cardo, what's up?" Romy said as he accepted the call. He waited, but there was no answer. "Cardo, did you butt dial me?" He waited again and this time he heard something. "Cardo, what's wrong?" he asked. He listened and heard the faint moan again. "Cardo!" he shouted.

"Romy," Cardo whispered. "Help me."

"What's wrong?"

"Don't... know. Stomach hurts."

Romy heard a clatter and pictured Cardo's phone hitting the floor. "Kit?" he called out and got no answer. "Shit!" Stabbing his finger at the touchpad, he called 911.

After giving the operator Cardo's location, Romy scribbled a note for Kit and left it on the refrigerator door. Jamming his feet into his boots, he hurried down the stairs and outside. Using the remote, he unlocked the

Ferrari and got in. As he drove, weaving through traffic, he called his mother. When her phone went to voicemail, he tried to call Kit, but got no answer. Dropping the phone on the seat beside him, Romy concentrated on getting to Cardo as quickly as possible. When he arrived, an ambulance was already there.

"Is he all right?" Romy asked one of the paramedics who was helping load an unconscious Cardo onto a gurney. "I'm his brother. I called you guys."

"Appendicitis," the paramedic said curtly. "Could you stand over there, please?"

"Will he be all right?"

"He'll have a better chance if you let us get him to the hospital."

"Where are you taking him?"

"St. Joseph."

"Thanks," Romy said as the two EMTs lifted the gurney and carried it out of the apartment. He brushed Cardo's hand with his as he stood aside. "You're going to be all right," he said. "I'm right behind you."

Romy got back in the car and called his mother again. This time she answered. "Finally," he said.

"I'm sorry, but it's a rule. We turn off our phones during club meetings."

"Okay. I knew that." Romy took a breath. "Mom, Cardo's being taken to the hospital. He has appendicitis."

"My God, no!"

"He's on his way to St. Joe's. Do you want me to come get you?"

"I'm at Mrs. Sarkissian's a couple of blocks away."

"Wait on the corner. I'll be there in a couple of minutes."

Actually, less than a minute went by before Romy was pulling up to the curb where his mother was standing. She got in quickly, and Romy drove away as she was fastening her seat belt.

"How did it happen?" she asked.

Romy shook his head. "He called me around ten thirty and sounded really sick, so I called 911. All I know is that the paramedics said Cardo has appendicitis."

"My poor baby." Mrs. O'Keefe began to cry.

Romy reached over and took one of her hands. "He's at the hospital getting treatment. Try not to worry too much."

"But he's so young."

"You wouldn't say that if you'd heard him giving me relationship advice earlier this evening."

"What's wrong with your relationship?" Mrs. O'Keefe asked, seizing on the distraction.

"I'm not sure it's going to work out with me and Kit."

"What? This is coming out of the blue."

"We're just too different and that's the bottom line. No matter how much we love each other, we're always going to run up against this wall eventually."

"What wall?"

"I can't give him what he needs."

"In what way?" Mrs. O'Keefe asked tentatively.

"Isn't it obvious? Look at this car. This is what he's used to."

"Honey, he's here with you. That's the important thing."

"I don't want him to make sacrifices to be with me. He'll end up resenting me."

"I think you're wrong, but why not deal with that when or if it ever comes up?"

"I can't, Mom. I can't lose anyone else."

"Well, you're going to, unless you go live alone on an island somewhere."

Romy pulled into the hospital parking lot and got out of the car. He waited for his mother to gather herself and then walked at her side into the emergency entrance. After few minutes of talking with a woman at a desk, she sent them into the warren of halls following one of the colored stripes on the floor. At their destination, a very compassionate nurse spoke with them and showed them where they could wait for the doctor.

"Can you tell us if he's all right?" Mrs. O'Keefe asked again.

"He's still in surgery, but they do this kind of operation all the time."

"Thank you." Mrs. O'Keefe sat down, crossed her ankles, and folded her hands in her lap.

Romy stood beside her chair, too anxious to sit. After about forty minutes, he asked his mom if she'd mind if he went outside for a while.

"I want to see if Kit called," he said. "And I can't turn the phone on in here."

"I'll be fine. Just don't be long, all right?"

"I won't."

Romy squeezed her hand and walked away down the corridor. As soon as he turned his phone on, it rang.

"Romy! Where are you?" Kit asked as soon as Romy answered.

"I'm at St. Joseph's hospital near my mom's. Cardo had an appendicitis attack and had to have surgery."

"Shit!"

"Yeah." Romy paused. "I took your car."

"I don't care about that."

"I'll be home as soon as I know Cardo's okay."

"Fuck that. I'm coming down there."

"You don't have to."

"I don't have to? Fuck you. I care about Cardo, too."

"Do what you want. You will anyway." Romy hit the *end call* button.

TWENTY-THREE

"WELL? HOW is he?" Kit asked when he finally found Romy and Mrs. O'Keefe in the office where they'd been asked to wait.

"He came through the surgery fine," Mrs. O'Keefe said. "He's in recovery now, and the surgeon said he's doing really well."

"Thank God." Kit visibly relaxed. "I was so worried."

Mrs. O'Keefe took Kit's hand. "The worst is over," she said and then turned her head as the office door opened.

"Hello," said the man who entered. "I'm Mr. Gault," he said. "I'm here to help you deal with the paperwork." He put a folder on the table and sat on one of the wooden chairs. "This won't take long, I promise."

"What are these?" Mrs. O'Keefe asked as Mr. Gault began taking papers from the folder and laying them out.

"Since Ricardo O'Keefe's appendix actually burst as he was brought in, the surgery was performed right away as a life-saving procedure, but we'd still like to have your signature on the permission form. We'd also like to know how you'll be paying."

"How much?" Romy asked.

"Well, we won't have the final figure until the end of Mr. O'Keefe's stay, but the surgery and associated services will be at least twenty-five thousand. Of course, this kind of thing is covered under most health insurance policies."

"That's nice," Romy said, but swallowed the rest of his reply when his mother looked up at him.

"Well, I think that does it for now," Mr. Gault said as he gathered the papers and stood. "I'm glad the young man is recovering."

After the administrator left, Romy's whole body sagged, and he covered his face with his hands as tears poured down. Mrs. O'Keefe put her hands on her son's shoulders and spoke softly to him.

"It's not the end of the world," she said.

"I'm sorry," Romy said in a voice thick with emotion. "It was just the last straw. Where are we going to get twenty-five thousand dollars... plus?"

"I could get the money," Kit said.

Romy and Mrs. O'Keefe turned to look at Kit.

"I could get the money," Kit repeated.

"Just stay out of it," Romy said. "This is family business."

Kit blinked. "All right," he said.

"And where would you get the money anyway?" Romy asked, his voice rising in volume. "Are you going to take Young up on his offer? Is that what you talked about when you called him? Did you go out to meet him?"

Kit was so shocked by the words and the pain in Romy's voice that he couldn't answer.

"It's okay," Romy continued. "You're used to a certain lifestyle, and he can provide that. I get it. I really do."

Kit shook his head, still unable to speak as his chest felt like it was being crushed, cutting off his breath.

"Just go. Get out," Romy said.

"Kit." Mrs. O'Keefe put a hand on Kit's forearm. "Would you drive me home?"

Kit looked down at her. "You want to go home?" he said numbly.

"Yes. Cardo is fine and needs to sleep. As do we all. If Romy doesn't want to come with us, he doesn't have to. Will you give me a ride?"

"Of course I'll give you a ride," Kit said. He looked at Romy. "You've got it wrong. Can we talk about this later?"

"I don't know. Can we?" Romy turned away. "I guess we'll see."

"Romy, please—" Kit's voice choked off.

"Kit," Mrs. O'Keefe said sharply. "We should go now."

"Yes, ma'am," Kit said automatically. When Mrs. O'Keefe went to the door, he moved to open it for her. Before he knew it, he was in the pale-green limbo of the hospital corridor. Guided by the sonar of Mrs. O'Keefe's heels clicking on the linoleum, he made it to the elevator on autopilot. His mind was consumed by thoughts of the angry exchange he'd had with Romy, and he was surprised to find himself getting into his car. How had he gotten here? He didn't remember getting out of the elevator or crossing the hospital lobby and the parking lot.

"Kit," Mrs. O'Keefe said. "I know it hurts, but leaving Romy alone for a while is the best thing you can do for him right now."

"Are you sure?"

"I know my son. Let him cry in private first and get it out of his system."

Kit started the engine and pulled away from the hospital. He forced himself to concentrate on driving and got Mrs. O'Keefe safely to her apartment. Once there, he couldn't refuse her request that he come in for a few minutes.

"I'm sorry Romy was so cruel to you," Mrs. O'Keefe said as she set a teacup in front of Kit.

"What happened?" Kit asked. "Can you tell me? Because I'm damned if I understand what just happened."

Mrs. O'Keefe hesitated and then made her decision. Life as a homosexual was not what she would have chosen for her son, but at least Romy had found someone to love who loved him back. That was no small thing in her estimation, and Romy wasn't going to lose Kit if there was something she could do about it.

"I know you love my Romy," she said. "And that you'd never hurt him on purpose, so I'm going to tell you some things he'd probably rather I didn't."

"I won't—"

"You won't tell on me?" Mrs. O'Keefe smiled slightly. "Don't worry. If he gets mad at me, I'll live through it."

"I've never seen him really mad," Kit said. "He's just so calm, you know? He takes things in stride, as my dad would say."

"He absorbs everything, that's true, and it's one of the reasons I worry about him. You haven't seen it yet, but there are times when he broods. It's like being near a black hole. When he's like that, nothing you can do or say will make him react. Twice in his life, I was afraid every day that he was going to… do something to himself."

"Tell me," Kit requested. "Tell me, so I can take better care of him."

"My husband left right after Cardo was born, just a few days before Romy's tenth birthday. He was very straightforward about it, no sneaking away. He very methodically packed all his things, put them out in the hall, and came back in to tell me he was leaving me. I asked him why, and he said that it just wasn't working out for him. He thought that a wife and children would make him happy, but he wasn't happy. He was going back to his hometown and back to playing the piano in sleazy bars. He didn't use the word sleazy. I added that."

Kit nodded, but didn't speak, not wanting to inhibit the flow of her words.

"I didn't realize Romy was listening until after my husband had gone. Romy came over to where I was sitting on the couch with Cardo in my arms and asked me if Daddy was playing a joke. I could see in his eyes that he knew his father wasn't joking, but he had to ask. He told me later that he wanted to run after him and beg him to stay, but he didn't want to leave me and Cardo alone."

Tears stung Kit's eyes, and he blinked them away. "I'm sorry," he said softly.

"It gets worse." Mrs. O'Keefe took another drink of tea. "I was left in the middle of a big city with two children and less than fifty dollars and no one to ask for help. I was an orphan, and if I have any family, I don't know about them." She took a deep breath. "After three days went by and Paul didn't return, I left Cardo with Romy and went looking for work. A restaurant on the block needed someone in the kitchen, and I took the job, working from seven in the morning to seven at night. They gave me money under the table, and it was just enough to pay for a cheap apartment and electricity. I brought home food from the restaurant, so we didn't have it so bad. And it was such a blessing that Romy was old enough to look after Cardo."

Mrs. O'Keefe took a sip of her tea and made a little face when she found it had grown cold. Kit got up and poured her a fresh cup while she talked.

"The lady across the hall took Cardo during the morning, but as soon as Romy got home from school, he took care of his little brother. When I got home from work, he would take whatever I'd brought with me into the kitchen and warm it up. He never ate until he'd brought plates to me and Cardo. After dinner, he'd do the washing up and bring me a big bowl of hot water to soak my feet. And he never complained, not once, about the things he couldn't have because we were so poor. I had thought that he might be bitter and blame me for his father leaving, but he didn't. Even as a teenager, he was remarkably accepting of hardship. He never had tantrums. He just quietly went to work on whatever the problem was. My little man.

"He got his first job when he was twelve. He got up early and delivered papers before school. Once he saw how money could add up if you put a little bit away every week, he went into high gear. He was always on the lookout for an opportunity. He'd deliver groceries, wash cars, weed gardens. He'd ride his bike to the loading docks and buy boxes of bubble gum right off the trucks and then sell the packs in the schoolyard for less than the corner store charged. By the time he was fourteen, he was supporting us and telling me I should quit working." She smiled. "I remember thinking he'd be a big business tycoon someday."

"I had no idea," Kit said. "I knew Romy hadn't had an easy life, but...." He shook his head. "I'm really sorry bad things happened to you, but for what it's worth, I think you did a great job raising your kids."

"Well, Romy practically raised Cardo, but thank you."

"I can picture this skinny kid pedaling his bike like crazy with a big box of bubble gum strapped to the back fender."

"He *was* skinny. Everything he ate went directly to fueling the machine, and he never gained any weight. Also, he insisted on wearing baggy shirts and shorts and high-top sneakers. For a year, he looked like a floppy kite made out of bendy straws. And his hair! He was always doing something different to it. One week it would be standing straight up, and the next it would be combed down to his eyebrows and have blond tips. But it was his only rebellion, so I didn't make a big deal out of it. Sometimes I think that maybe I should have. Maybe he wanted me to be shocked and tell him he couldn't dye his hair. Maybe he wanted me to get angry and shout at him. Maybe I would have found out sooner that he blamed himself when Paul left us."

"No."

Mrs. O'Keefe nodded. "When Romy was sixteen, he told me he knew why his father had left and never contacted us again. He thought it was because of him. 'If I'd been a better son, Dad would have been happy and stayed with us.' Those were Romy's exact words. I've never forgotten them. My heart broke to think that Romy had felt that way for six years and I'd never noticed. What kind of mother was I?"

Kit put a hand over hers. "A good one," he said.

Mrs. O'Keefe blotted her tears with her napkin. "I'm sorry, but it breaks my heart again each time I think about Romy blaming himself. He felt he'd failed me and Cardo by not going after Paul and bringing him back."

"I can't imagine carrying all that guilt around so young."

"Things were better after he talked with me. I could see that he still felt bad about it, but a lot of the weight was gone from his shoulders. He was a senior in high school, and he was finally able to enjoy being a teenager." Mrs. O'Keefe paused. "I think I'm going to need more tea to tell the next part." She paused again. "If you want to hear it."

"I want to know everything I can about Romy," Kit said as he made two more cups of tea. "The more I know, the better I can understand."

"And he's not exactly a blabbermouth, is he?"

"No, ma'am." Kit set a cup in front of Mrs. O'Keefe and sat back down.

"I just hope he doesn't get too angry with me for blabbing, but it's partly my story too." Mrs. O'Keefe smiled wistfully into her tea. "You've seen his graduation picture, so you know what he looked like back then. My beautiful boy. Once he got rid of the baggy clothes and became more social, the girls started to notice him. He started dating a girl from his art class. Her name was Aletha, and she was a real piece of work."

Kit looked up at the tone of Mrs. O'Keefe's voice, but he didn't speak.

"Aletha seemed like a sweet girl at first. She was a little different, of course. Arty, you know? She wore black tights and she dyed her bangs purple, which was what attracted Romy in the first place. I believed her innocent act right up until the day she told Romy she was pregnant."

"You're kidding!"

Mrs. O'Keefe shook her head. "He asked her to marry him, of course. I didn't want to give my consent, but he convinced me it was the best thing to do, and he was going to be eighteen in a few weeks anyway and wouldn't need my permission. I resigned myself to helping raise my grandchild, but Aletha turned down the proposal. She didn't want to get married, and she certainly didn't want to have a baby at sixteen. What she wanted was money for an abortion and a train ticket to a clinic in another town."

"What did Romy do?"

"He did his best to talk her into marrying him, but her mind was made up. I'll confess that I took her side in the argument. Having seen her true colors, I wanted her out of my son's life as fast as possible. Romy finally saw that Aletha wasn't going to budge, and he gave in. I advised him to give her the money out of our savings. It took almost all of what we had, but it was worth it to me. We found out later that she used the money to go on a honeymoon with the twenty-year-old man who was the real father of her baby."

"Not really?" Kit cleared his throat. "Sorry. I don't think you're making this up, but how could that girl have been so coldhearted?"

"I've learned that all people have reasons for what they do, even if I don't understand them. Who knows why Aletha treated Romy that way? Maybe she's out there somewhere eaten up with remorse about it. I don't know. I only know that she shredded Romy's heart when she left him. The next time we heard anything about Aletha, her mother-in-law was showing baby pictures to friends in the restaurant where I worked. The last time we heard about her, she was the hot gossip for running away with a rock musician, leaving her husband and one-year-old daughter behind.

"When I told Romy about it, he didn't say anything. His expression didn't even change. He just left for his night job like always. But it was another six months before he started acting like himself instead of a zombie. He was cracking jokes again, spending time with Cardo, taking a course in auto mechanics. I was disappointed when he didn't want to go to college, but he'd been making decisions for himself for a long time. If fixing cars makes him happy, why shouldn't he do that?" She met Kit's eyes. "And if you make him happy, why shouldn't he have you?"

"You're going to make me cry. Again." Kit took her hands in his. "But thanks for saying that. I wish *my* mom felt the same way."

"She probably has her reasons. I'm sure she loves you, no matter what your differences are."

"I miss her." Kit swallowed. "I miss my sisters. I miss my whole family. I even miss Dad bullying me."

"I'm sorry." Mrs. O'Keefe squeezed Kit's fingers. "I'd like to think of you as a son, if you don't mind."

Kit swallowed again. "I'd be honored," he said. "And thank you for… everything."

Mrs. O'Keefe smiled. "I don't want you to think Romy's life was nothing but heartbreak. He had friends. He went to amusement parks and concerts. When he was fifteen, he took second place in a competition where he did stunts with bicycles. He scared me half to death sometimes, but I was always proud of him, and I made sure he knew it."

"I envy him that." Kit looked down and back up again. "When did he start liking boys?"

"I'm not sure it ever made a difference to him if the person he liked was male or female, but I've never asked."

"I guess I'll have to ask him." Kit let go of her hands. "I should go. I've grilled you unmercifully, and even if Romy's going to be grumpy, I want to be with him."

"You understand now, don't you? He's not angry with you. He's just feeling like he's letting everyone down." Mrs. O'Keefe stood when Kit did and walked him to the door.

"I understand. I won't throw my imaginary wealth around again."

"You didn't do anything wrong. It was a very sweet, kind, and generous gesture."

"Too bad it was an empty one." Kit gave her a wry smile. "Thanks for the tea."

"No sincere offer of help is ever truly empty. Any impulse toward kindness is good for the soul."

"Thank you. I'll call you and let you know how things go."

CHAPTER
TWENTY-FOUR

KIT DROVE back to the hospital and parked. He sat there for a while as he made some phone calls. The last one was to Romy. He was greatly relieved when Romy answered.

"Where are you?" Romy asked.

"In the hospital parking lot."

"Which one?"

"Which hospital?"

"The hospital has three parking lots. Which one are you in?"

"Oh. I found a spot by the emergency room. Where are you?"

"I'm out by the trash compactors in the back."

"Stay there. I'll drive around."

"Okay." Romy hung up.

"I didn't know you smoked," Kit said as he drove up beside Romy.

Romy tossed his cigarette into a puddle. "I quit a couple of years ago." He got into the passenger seat. "I cadged that one off an orderly who told me where I could smoke in peace."

"I'm not making any judgments."

"I wasn't insinuating that you were."

"Sorry. I'm a little jumpy."

"That's my fault." Romy looked out the rain-streaked windshield. "I'm really sorry I yelled at you. I said horrible things to you on purpose to hurt you."

"You were on edge. I shouldn't have—"

"Don't," Romy interrupted. "Don't make excuses for me. No matter what I was going through, you didn't deserve that." He dropped his head to his chest. "I don't expect you to forgive me."

"Of course I forgive you."

"You'll have to pardon me if I don't forgive myself."

"You'd better. I'll pester you until you do, and you know how persistent I can be."

Romy's gaze shifted over to Kit. "I shouldn't have said that thing about Brandis."

"No, you shouldn't have, but let it drop, okay? I can tell you that I'll never be unfaithful to you, but until you trust me, it's just words. However, I'm going to prove to you that I don't want anyone else, even if it takes the rest of my life. I love you."

"I guess I'm just slow to believe."

"I know you can't believe that someone could love you, but I'm not kidding. I'm going to be here every day of your life proving it to you."

"That sounds like a threat."

"Just don't make me mad. You won't like me when I'm mad."

"Angry," Romy said. "The quote is, you won't like me when I'm *angry*."

"Do you have any self-preservation instincts at all?"

"I'm a real bite in the ass, huh?"

"Is that an offer?"

"Kit…." Romy sighed heavily. "I appreciate what you're doing, but I need to wallow in my shortcomings for a while, okay?"

"No, not really." Kit smiled when he surprised a laugh out of Romy. "But like I said, I love you, and that means I love you no matter what mood you're in. I might not like it, but I won't leave you just because you lose your temper once a year."

"You mean that, don't you?" Romy said in a tone of wonder.

"Yes, I do. When I say I love you, I mean I love all of you and everything that comes with you. Your troubles are my troubles. Your happiness is my happiness. Your family is my family. And so on. You get my point."

"I hope you know I feel the same way."

Kit chuckled. "I think I'm getting the better end of this deal in the family department."

"Hey, at least they bought you this cool car." Romy smiled at Kit.

"That reminds me, you should say good-bye to her."

"Why?"

"I sold her."

"What? When?"

"About an hour ago."

"Why would you do that?"

"I told you I could raise the money. As it turns out, I was telling the truth."

"You can't sell your car to pay Cardo's hospital bill."

"I already did, and there'll be quite a bit left over."

"I can't let you."

"How are you going to stop me?" Kit pulled into the parking lot of an all-night diner.

"I won't accept the money."

"Then I'll give it to your mom. Don't argue. I'm family, remember? This is what family does."

"But you love this car," Romy said as he stroked the elegant line of the dashboard.

"No, *you* love this car. Me, I think it's pretty, and it gets me quickly from one place to another while looking damn sexy, but I don't have actual feelings for it." Kit opened his door. "Believe me, it's not as hard as you might think for me to give it up."

"You know Cardo's going to kill you, right?" Romy said as he got out. "He'll never forgive you for sacrificing the Ferrari for him."

"I'll have to live with that." Kit pushed through the door of the diner. "Honestly, I can't imagine why I didn't think of it before. I don't need a Ferrari, and it's worth a certain amount of money. Why not sell it?" He grinned over his shoulder at Romy.

"You rich kids," Romy said with mock disgust. "You think you can solve any problem with money." He paused. "Actually, there are a lot of problems that *can* be solved with money."

"At least most of the little ones. You still can't buy love."

"For which, as a poor man, I am mightily grateful." Romy sat down in a booth, and Kit slid in across the table from him.

A waitress brought menus and returned to pour coffee. Kit and Romy ordered waffles and an omelet respectively, and the waitress refilled their cups before she left.

"I can't believe this song is playing." Kit looked toward the ceiling. "It was playing in the car just before the engine died on the day I met you. Weird."

"Do we need an exorcist?" Romy joked.

"No, it's a good weird. It reminds me that you never know what's around the corner."

"I don't recognize it." Romy looked up too as though the name of the song might be written on the ceiling.

"It's 'I Need a Forever Lover.' You really don't recognize it?"

Romy shook his head. "But if it's going to be our song, I'll get familiar with it."

"No!" Kit laughed. "It's a silly, flavor-of-the-month pop song. We haven't found our song yet. Unless it's the lullaby you sang me when I was hurt. I always meant to ask you about it."

"Because it was so crappy, right? I wrote it when I was fourteen. When Cardo was little, he was scared of storms. He could never sleep if it was thundering. So when I wanted Cardo to go to bed, I sang to him, and sometimes, I made the songs up."

"I want to hear all of them."

Romy looked down as he shook his head. "It would be too humiliating," he said. "Why don't I write one just for you and sing that one?"

"How long will it take?"

"Can you put a time limit on creativity?"

"That was sneaky," Kit said as the waitress arrived with the food.

The young woman filled their coffee cups again, asked if they needed anything else, anything at all, and told them she'd be right over there if they did find they needed something else.

"Great service here," Kit said as the waitress walked away.

Romy reached across the table and took a syrup-dripping forkful of Kit's waffles. He chewed and swallowed. "Great waffles too," he said. "Try the omelet?"

Kit tasted the omelet and pronounced it good. "I'm glad we're not fighting," he said.

"I'm not sure how to act. It blew up so fast. I thought you were gone for good."

"But I'm still here."

A slow smile spread over Romy's face. "You are, aren't you? Sitting right across from me eating waffles with a revolting amount of syrup and being nice to me."

"More cream?" the waitress said at Kit's elbow. She held up a small jug.

"Thanks," Kit said as she refreshed his coffee again.

"He likes cream," Romy said with a straight face.

"There's plenty more," she said.

"Yeah, cream is kind of self-renewing, isn't it?"

"Yeah, I guess you could say that. Can I bring you anything else? Do you have enough sugar?"

"Plenty," Kit said. "Thank you."

The waitress went back to the counter and wiped it down while stealing looks at the occupied booth.

"I think she has a crush on you," Romy said.

"No, she's watching you. You were the one saying suggestive things to her."

"You're gorgeous. I'm a wreck."

"You're a sexy wreck. Now, finish your breakfast, you're going to need the energy."

"I wish I could kiss you right now."

Kit looked around. "We're the only ones in here," he said, grinning impishly.

"As I've often observed, you're a lunatic."

"I dare you."

Romy leaned across the table, and Kit met him halfway for a quick kiss.

"Someday," Kit said as he settled back in his seat. "Someday, we'll be able to do that without looking both ways first."

"You want to move to San Francisco?"

"Do you think your mom would like San Francisco?"

Romy chuckled, but before he could reply, the waitress was back. "I don't mean to bug you guys," she said. "You can sit as long as you want. I was just wondering…."

"How can we help you?" Romy asked.

"Well, it's a little personal, but I was wondering if you're a couple."

"Why do you ask?"

"Well…. I just thought you might be, and I wanted to see if I was right. Because if you are, I want you to know that you're the cutest couple that's ever been in here."

"That's not what I was expecting," Romy said. "Thank you."

"Yeah, thanks," Kit said. "So, you really think we're cute?"

"You're both dreamy." The waitress giggled. "I'm going to feel like such a fool tomorrow, but I just had to tell you."

"No, it's really sweet," Kit said. "We should be going, though, so if we could have the check…."

"You can pay at the register," she said and met him there. "I hope you two have a really great life together," she said as Kit told her to keep the change. "Not because you're a big tipper. Because I can see in your eyes how much you love each other. I can tell about these things, and I know you're going to be together for a long time."

"Thanks," Kit said. He met Romy at the door and told him what the waitress had said.

"Maybe that day is coming sooner than we think," Romy said. "Maybe we won't have to move to San Francisco, after all."

CHAPTER

TWENTY-FIVE

KIT COLLAPSED on Romy's sweat-dewed back and panted heavily as his climax reverberated throughout his body. "Holy hell, that was good," he said.

Romy stretched as far as he was able in his position. "It sure was a sweet ride," he agreed in a scratchy voice.

"How is it possible that it keeps getting better?" Kit kissed his way down Romy's spine, pausing to trace the little sun tattoo with his tongue.

"Because we keep getting to know each other better?"

"Sounds like a plausible theory." Gently Kit disengaged and reached over the side of the bed for the towel. He offered it to Romy before flopping onto his back. "Why can't I ever remember to bump the air conditioning down when we fuck?"

"We didn't exactly plan this." Romy stretched out against Kit's side and stroked his chest. "It's the middle of the day. I should be working."

As if his words were a cue, his phone rang.

"Shit," Romy said. "Why can't I remember to turn off my phone when we're fucking?"

Kit laughed as he handed Romy's phone to him. As Romy answered, Kit got up and went into the bathroom. Kit got in the shower long enough to rinse off the layer of sweat and went back to bed.

"Thanks again, man," Romy said. "Yeah, I'll see you then." He looked up at Kit and grinned. "I have a job!"

"You're not looking for a job, I am."

"Babe, we've been talking about how slow business is. It'll be easy for me to work somewhere else and do repairs at night."

"We also talked about how we have quite a bit of money left over even after all of Cardo's hospital bills were paid."

"That's our savings. We're not using it to live on." Romy paused. "I didn't mean for that to sound like a royal command."

"No? Because that's exactly what it sounded like."

"You know how I get when it comes to money."

"Yes, but we're going to cure you of that someday." Kit settled against the pillows and put his arms around Romy. "So what's the job?"

"Remember when we first started dating—"

"You mean four months ago? Yeah, I can remember that far back."

"Whatever. Remember the time you sent that car for me? Well, the driver felt like he owed me because I fixed something on the limo. Anyway, he just told me about a job that came up at the limo company. They need a mechanic to maintain their fleet, and the job comes with a salary and benefits. Plus, since I have a chauffeur's license already, I can pick up extra money by driving when they're really busy."

"It sounds good." Kit tilted his head to look into Romy's eyes. "But if you take this job you have to promise me one thing."

"Anything."

"If they give you a uniform, wear the hat and boots when you come home."

"My pleasure."

"It certainly will be."

"Love you, babe, even if you are a sex-crazed lunatic." Romy smirked.

"I thought you loved me *because* I'm a sex-crazed lunatic."

Romy's phone rang again. "Suddenly I'm Mr. Popular."

"At least they waited until we were done screwing," Kit said as Romy accepted the call.

Romy laughed. "No, Mom," he said. "Kit just said something funny."

"Tell her I said hi," Kit said.

"Kit says hi," Romy said as Kit got out of bed. "Where are you going? No, sorry, Mom, I was talking to Kit. Just a sec, okay?" He put the phone down and went to hug Kit from behind. "You getting dressed?"

"Might as well. I think playtime is over for now." Kit turned in the circle of Romy's arms to kiss him. "I'm going to make a snack." He kissed Romy again and left the room to let Romy finish his conversation.

By the time Romy joined Kit in the kitchen, Kit had made a spinach salad and eaten a good portion of it. He handed Romy a fork, and they ate out of the same big bowl.

"How's Mom?" Kit asked, openly ogling Romy's treasure trail where it dove under the waistband of his low-hanging jeans.

"She's great. Cardo's great. He wants to get out and do things like play basketball and of course, he can't yet. I think Mom's tired of being the bad guy who has to tell him no. Anyway, I'm going over and talk with him tonight or tomorrow. I know it sucks being laid up, but he doesn't need to give her a hard time."

"Surgery is for sure a no-fun activity. We could cook dinner and take it over," Kit said.

"Let's plan on doing that tomorrow night, then."

"Okay, but it'll have to be tomorrow or wait another day. We have plans for Friday night, remember? My friends and your friends getting together to see who can embarrass us the most."

"Yeah, good times."

"You know what I think?"

"I wouldn't even try to guess."

"I think Cardo's appendicitis was the last calamity. I think from now on things are going up, up, up." Kit kissed Romy. "Just wait and see."

ASIDE FROM the ordinary obstacles that everyday life throws in everyone's path, Kit's prophecy proved to be a true one. The limo company was very pleased with Romy's work, and he received regular raises. Kit found a part-time job at a gym a few blocks from the apartment. They managed to start saving money from their paychecks, while still helping Romy's family. Kit's sisters ganged up on his father, and he grudgingly gave his wife permission to see her son. Life really was getting better all the time. And then one day at an employee-appreciation party, Kit saw something that inspired him.

"What's in the back?" Kit asked as Romy was giving him a tour of the limo company's facility.

"Bored already?"

"No, a huge building full of long black cars thrills me to the bone."

"It's not that bad. You liked the buffet."

"Yes, I did. The employees here are treated really well. That food was top-notch and not too frou-frou."

"There's a company policy about frou-frou."

"Well, I'm not saying a little frou-frou wouldn't be nice, but you know how I feel about pretentiousness."

"Yeah, you're a regular Holden Caulfield."

"Keep up the sweet talk and you could get lucky."

"Why don't I show you what's out back?"

Kit craned his neck until he could see Romy's ass. "I can see what's out back, and I like it. That's why I'm looking for a place with some privacy."

"Come on," Romy said as he pushed open a heavy swinging door. "I'm sure Mr. Saltillo won't mind."

"What won't I mind?" A man's voice came from the left as Romy and Kit stepped through the doorway.

"Mr. Saltillo!" Romy said. "I'm sorry if we disturbed you."

"Don't worry about it. I can do this whenever I like." Mr. Saltillo gestured with his cigar at the antique car gleaming softly in the center of the room. "Sometimes I like to just look at her."

"It's beautiful!" Kit exclaimed. "What is it?"

"A 1926 Daimler-Benz," Mr. Saltillo said. "The first car they built after Daimler and Benz merged. Take a closer look if you like."

Romy and Kit went over with Mr. Saltillo, and the elderly man pointed out features of the car. Kit was very taken with the upholstery and the fittings, especially the silver filigree bud vases on either side of the back doors.

"It's like a work of art," Kit said. "People knew how to travel in style back then."

"You sound very sensible for someone your age." Mr. Saltillo puffed on his cigar. "But I've held you up long enough. What were you two young men up to when I stopped you?"

"I was just going to show Kit what we keep out back."

"If you were a couple, I'd suspect you were sneaking off to neck." Mr. Saltillo chuckled.

Romy hesitated, exchanged a glance with Kit, and cleared his throat. "Actually, sir, we are a couple."

"The hell you say!"

"I'm not pulling your leg. We're in love and we live together and everything."

"But… you're such a good mechanic," Mr. Saltillo said.

"Thank you."

Mr. Saltillo thought for a minute. "That's the damnedest thing," he said. "You mean to tell me you can be a homo *and* work on cars?"

"Yep, just like a real man," Romy said.

"Wasn't like that when I was growing up. A sissy was a sissy and that was that."

"Times change, I guess," Kit said.

"Yes, they do," Mr. Saltillo said. "It's a good thing and a bad thing. I'm all for progress, but so many little niceties get lost along the way."

"You should come to one of Kit's afternoon teas," Romy said before he thought about it. "Excuse me, sir. I don't know why I said that."

"I'm not offended. Why would I be?"

"I think he thought you'd think he was being sassy about the gay thing," Kit said.

"Ah, I see." Mr. Saltillo put his cigar to his lips and blew a smoke ring. "Honestly, you can be as gay as you want as long as the cars are taken care of. Especially my baby."

"It's a pleasure keeping her in trim," Romy said.

Mr. Saltillo glanced between Romy and Kit and shook his head. "It's the damnedest thing," he said. "You were gay all this time, and I never knew." He chuckled.

"Us gays are like that," Romy said. "We're so much like normal people that you can't tell the difference sometimes."

"*Now* you're being sassy," Mr. Saltillo said. "Go ahead and finish showing the place to your boyfriend or husband or whatever the right word is." He chuckled again. "Rascal."

"Good night, sir."

"Nice to meet you," Kit said. "Anytime you want to come to tea, let me know." He smiled. "Of course, after the first cup, the tea is actually scotch or bourbon, depending on tastes."

"Come on." Romy took Kit's arm and pulled him away. "Whew," Romy said when they were out of earshot. "I almost shat myself."

"Why? I thought your boss was really nice." Kit interlaced his fingers with Romy's. "And I can't tell you how proud I am of you."

"I'm just glad you aren't pissed off."

"Of course not, and anyway, you owed me one for outing you to my family."

"I wasn't even thinking about that," Romy protested.

Kit laughed. "I'm teasing you, dick-brain."

Romy smacked the back of Kit's head. "And I'm smacking you."

"You'll pay for that."

Romy took off with Kit at his heels, hitting the bar of the outside door just a step ahead. His foot slipped on loose gravel and Kit caught him.

"Vengeance is mine," Kit said as he tweaked Romy's nose.

Letting go of his boyfriend, Kit looked around the large outdoor area that was surrounded by a high fence. Along the side of the building on a concrete slab, protected by a long awning, sat several picnic tables and a couple of trough-like ashtrays filled with sand. Around the inside of the fence, he saw a row of oleander trees and in the far corner, a bulky shape overgrown with weeds. It was the first untidy thing Kit had seen on the property, and it piqued his curiosity.

"What's over there?" he asked.

"It's a car Mr. Saltillo bought to restore."

"Is it like the one inside?" Kit asked as he headed over.

"Well, it's not the same make, model, or year, but in a way, it is."

"I mean is it an antique limo?"

"It's a 1939 Rolls-Royce Phantom."

Kit parted the weeds and Romy helped lift a corner of the canvas tarp so they could see in the car's side window. Though in poor shape, the Rolls was definitely salvageable given enough money and hard work. Letting the canvas drop back into place, Kit stared into the middle distance, while tapping a finger against his lips.

Romy was by now familiar with this expression and didn't say anything until Kit looked at him. "So watcha thinkin'?"

"Would Mr. Saltillo sell this car?"

"I doubt it. Why?"

"I just had an idea for a business."

Romy watched Kit talk, entranced by the light in his lover's eyes.

"At most of the weddings I've been to, the bride and groom arrive in a car like this that a grandfather or great-uncle loaned them. But what if you don't know anyone with a Rolls or a Bentley?"

"There are already businesses that rent limos for weddings."

"What I want to do is a full-on party cruise, land-yacht style."

"Tell me more."

"It would be like a party tour of the city with a handsome driver and a host maybe to serve gourmet snacks and pour drinks. We'd have themes and decorate the car accordingly. The driver and host can wear costumes. We can have Victorian outings, Roaring Twenties jazz hops, Magical Mystery tours. You name it."

"And you can organize all this?"

"I'm gay. Of course I can plan a party," Kit scoffed.

"Well, I *do* have a chauffeur's license."

"And you're sex on wheels in that uniform. So, what do you think?"

"I think you're right. I'm sex on wheels."

Kit punched Romy's shoulder.

"Well," Romy said. "I think an antique Rolls is going to be spendy."

"Do we have enough money to fix this one up, and would that be cheaper than buying one?"

"It would be cheaper to restore this one since I'd be donating my labor, but I really don't think he'll sell it."

"Would it hurt to talk to him?"

"I guess not."

"Then let's go see if he'll even talk about it."

They found Mr. Saltillo where they'd left him and broached the subject of buying the Rolls. As Romy had predicted, his boss was reluctant.

"The only reason I haven't done anything with her is that the company is doing so well. I like doing the work myself, but I just haven't had the time." Mr. Saltillo frowned in thought. "I think your idea is a good one, and I can see you're enthusiastic about it. Would you consider a counterproposal?"

"I'd be happy to hear one," Kit said.

"Suppose I sell you half the car? I'll even help finance the restoration. My conditions are that Romy continues to work here until he can find or train a replacement, and I'm a partner in the party business."

"You mean it?" Kit asked excitedly.

"Your passion is very persuasive," Mr. Saltillo said. "Romy is one of my favorite employees, and I'd like to see him do well. And damn it, a venture like this is just what a man needs to keep his blood stirred up."

"Thank you," Kit said. "I have a really good feeling about this."

"It's funny, but so do I," Mr. Saltillo said. "Half an hour ago, I'd never have considered getting into bed with a homosexual, but after finding out—" He stopped talking at the sound of Romy and Kit's snickering. "I said something funny?" He went back over his words and a grin spread over his face. "Yes, I guess I did." He chuckled. "It's just an expression, you know."

"What a shame," Kit said cheekily.

Mr. Saltillo chuckled again. "As I was saying, finding out that Romy is… well, you know, *gay*, has made me think. So, I'm going to take a chance." He took a deep breath and let it out again. "It's good to be alive, isn't it? With a new project waiting and optimism in your heart?"

"Yeah, it is," Romy agreed.

"Come in a little early on Monday, and we'll settle some details about the car. Kit, you're included in this meeting, of course."

"I have work," Kit said. "And I trust Romy to make decisions about the car."

"Just the car?" Romy raised his eyebrows.

"Yes, dear, just the car."

Mr. Saltillo laughed. "Keep your eye on this one, Romy," he said. "He's sharp."

"Don't worry, sir. I'm onto him."

"Speaking of that, we should get home," Kit said. "I have to open the gym tomorrow, and you know how the early birds get if they have to wait for two seconds."

"Hell hath no fury like a weight lifter on steroids," Romy joked.

"Good night, then," Mr. Saltillo said.

Kit and Romy said good night and walked back through the cavernous garage. After saying their good-byes to the other employees, they started for home.

"I love living within walking distance of work," Kit said as they strolled along.

"It's not exactly a scenic route." Romy gestured at the industrial park that surrounded them.

"It's not so bad. At least there's some landscaping. It's not all concrete."

"You always insist on seeing the bright side. It's really getting on my nerves."

"You ain't seen nothin' yet."

Romy caught Kit's swinging hand and interlaced their fingers. "You sure charmed the hell out of my boss."

"He's a nice man. I think most people are nice if you give them a chance."

"Who told you that?"

"Your mom."

"Oh. Then it's probably true."

Kit squeezed Romy's hand. "I think a lot of people are like Mr. Saltillo. They don't know any gay people. If they did, they'd see we're just like everyone else. We want the same things. We want love and approval and to be able to live without fear."

"That about sums it up for me." Romy smiled. "Except the part where I want to throw you over my shoulder, run for home, and stuff you silly."

"Right," Kit said. "Just like everyone else."

"Oh no you didn't!" Romy exclaimed. "You conceited little—"

But Kit had already let go of Romy's hand and sprinted away from him. Romy chased Kit all the way home, both laughing like crazy and arriving completely out of breath. Yet they found the strength to make love before falling asleep together to dream the same dream. And when they woke, they started working together to make those dreams come true.

EPILOGUE

KIT RAN his fingers gently over the petals of a white rose. The rose was one of many that graced the interior of the limousine, along with sprays of ferns among clouds of white netting. Combined with the antique Rolls-Royce's elegant style, the decorations were the perfect backdrop for this occasion. He could be proud of the job he'd done.

"It's beautiful," Romy said as he stuck his head in the car door.

"Thanks. I always want the cars to look perfect, but today…." Kit's voice trailed off.

"I know. It's so hard to believe Cardo's getting married."

"Our little brother—" Kit's voice broke and Romy got into the car to put an arm around him.

"It doesn't seem possible he's twenty."

Kit rested his head on Romy's shoulder. "I'm so proud of him," he said.

Romy chuckled. "I don't know who's prouder, you or Mom."

"Well, he did graduate from college in three years instead of four."

"Yep. And he kept his promise not to get married until he finished school."

"He's an amazing kid. And I love his fiancée."

"Yeah, well, she's your niece."

Kit squeezed Romy. "It makes me so happy that both our families will be here today."

"Me, too."

"I don't want to jinx things, but it seems like we've been having really good luck for quite a while now. The business is doing so well, my dad doesn't hate me anymore, and I love you more every day." Kit kissed Romy's cheek. "I'm really lucky you saw through this spoiled brat and took a chance on him."

"I never thought of you as a spoiled brat."

"Oh, come on."

"Well, maybe at the beginning… the very beginning… for like, two seconds."

"What do you think of me now?" Kit asked coyly.

Romy took the question seriously and thought for a moment before he answered. "When I think of you, it's like, you know, when you're walking down a shady path and you see a patch of sunshine ahead, and then you step into the light. Suddenly everything that was ordinary is beautiful, and everything that was beautiful is divine."

Kit swallowed. "Yeah. Beauty is always there, but it's up to us to see it."

Romy kissed Kit's cheek. "Thanks for being my sunshine."

"I may puke."

Romy chuckled. "Go ahead. I'll even hold your hair for you."

"Romy. Kit," Mrs. O'Keefe called out as she approached the car. "Are you here?"

Kit and Romy got out on opposite sides of the car and greeted Mrs. O'Keefe with hugs.

"You're beautiful, Mom," Romy said.

"Really beautiful, Paloma," Kit said as he fussed with her corsage. "I can't wait to watch you give Cardo away."

"Such a silly idea," Mrs. O'Keefe said, but her eyes were sparkling.

"I don't think it's any sillier than giving the bride away," Kit said. "And this is my wedding, so—" He stopped talking when Romy and his mother cracked up. "Okay. Okay. I know it's Cardo and Jennifer's wedding, but…."

"We understand," Mrs. O'Keefe said. "And after all, you did plan the entire event." She smiled. "I hope one day it *will* be your wedding you're planning."

Kit kissed her cheek. "I couldn't ask for a better mother-in-law."

"What about you?" Romy teased his mother. "When are you getting married?"

"I have no idea what you're talking about," Mrs. O'Keefe said primly.

"Maybe you should ask your boyfriend," Romy said, looking over her shoulder.

"You're embarrassing me!"

"Who's embarrassing this lovely woman?" Mr. Saltillo said as he took Mrs. O'Keefe's arm.

"These two punks," Mrs. O'Keefe said.

"Punks?" Mr. Saltillo looked around. "Surely, you don't mean my esteemed partners."

"They were being very cheeky."

"I'd think you'd be used to it by now," Mr. Saltillo said. "I certainly am."

"Why do men always stick together?"

"Because we know we're no match for you on our own." Mr. Saltillo kissed Mrs. O'Keefe's cheek and made her blush. "People are asking where you are," he said to Kit and Romy.

"We should put in an appearance, I suppose." Kit patted his hair. "How do I look?"

"You look very handsome," Mrs. O'Keefe said, and Mr. Saltillo murmured agreement. "Young men look so good in those Victorian-style suits. You too, my son."

Romy didn't say anything, but the look in his eyes was enough for Kit.

"Let's join the guests, then," Kit said as he took Romy's hand.

A small crowd had gathered in the formal garden that flanked the right side of Vintage Voyages' event complex. The wedding guests stood about on the paths between the short hedges and beds of flowers or sat on chairs draped with snowy satin and adorned with sprays of ferns and white roses. Under an arch of white wicker covered with ivy and more white roses, stood Ricardo O'Keefe looking quite grown-up in a classic cutaway morning suit. Cardo broke off his conversation with the minister as Romy and Kit joined them.

"Man, just look at you," Romy said as he hugged Cardo.

"Careful," Kit said. "Don't crush the boutonnieres."

"Come here," Cardo said, pulling Kit into a hug. "Thank you both," Cardo said as he stepped back. "Thanks for standing with me today, and

Romy, thanks for standing with me every day of my life. You took care of me, stood up for me, and showed me how to be a man. I never needed a father. I had you."

Romy pressed his lips together until he gave up and let his tears fall. He put his arms around Cardo again and held him tightly before letting him go.

"I guess we're ready," Kit said.

"As ready as I'll ever be," Cardo said.

Kit smiled and turned to signal the ushers. Four of Cardo's friends from college went into action and got all the guests seated, before taking their places alongside the groom and the best man. Romy patted his jacket pocket, and then smiled as Kit handed him a small velvet-covered box. Kit gave another signal, the string quartet in the rose arbor began to play, and the wedding of Ricardo O'Keefe and Jennifer Britten-Lee was underway.

The ceremony was moving. The bride was beautiful. The groom was dashing. Tears dampened smiling faces as a sacred oath was taken and two people began a new life together. The couple turned to greet their guests as man and wife for the first time and the celebration began.

"Everything was just perfect," Mrs. O'Keefe said as Kit sat her and Mr. Saltillo at the head table. "All the decorations are so lovely."

"Indeed they are," Jackie said as she and Eliza rose to hug Kit. "You've done a magnificent job, little brother."

"Thank you," Kit said. "Your daughter is our most beautiful bride yet."

"She takes after her uncle," Jackie said. "The way Cardo takes after Paloma."

Kit stepped back and let the new in-laws talk. He bumped into Romy and turned to look up at him. "Are you stalking me?"

"Thought I'd already snared you."

"Yeah, well." Kit paused. After nearly five years together, Romy still managed to make him tongue-tied and anxious just by standing close to him. "Thinking's not your strong suit, is it?" As Kit had hoped, Romy pretended to be offended.

"You can tell I'm not too smart. Look who I ended up with."

Kit laughed. "I'm the one who stalked you."

"Just as I always suspected," Romy said. "You saw this body and had to have it."

"That's indisputable, but you have to admit that I showed remarkable restraint."

"You were a perfect gentleman." Romy looked around. "I guess it'd be rude to leave the party just so I can kiss you."

"Maybe just a little bit." Kit gave Romy a quick kiss on the cheek. "That'll have to do until we can be alone."

Romy sighed. "I'm still waiting for that day when I can kiss you in public without worrying about who's going to see us."

"It's coming," Kit said confidently. "Meanwhile, we have gay clubs and resorts where we can do whatever we want."

"True. So why the wistful look?"

"Well… I'm happy my mom is here, but I still wish my dad would come around."

"He will." Romy kissed Kit's forehead.

Kit and Romy broke off their conversation to greet a couple of guests who wanted to compliment the wedding. As the guests walked away, Romy looked around at the happy people celebrating his little brother's wedding.

"All we need is some rock 'n' roll," he said.

"I think the chamber music is a little more appropriate to the ambiance," Kit said.

"It doesn't exactly make you want to get up and dance."

"So you keep saying." Kit hummed along with the music as he watched Cardo waltz with Mrs. O'Keefe.

"Ash called this morning while you were at the flower market."

"I assume it wasn't anything urgent." Kit leaned his shoulder against Romy's. "Could you be any happier right now?" he asked as Jackie's husband took Romy's mother's hand and invited her to dance.

"I could be looking forward to seeing Joplin's band in concert on Saturday. Since Ash took over managing them, they've done really well."

Kit nodded. "Yes, they have. And Joplin and Ash make such a cute couple."

"Gag me. They're a terrible match. I can't believe they've been together almost two years. I've never seen two people so different."

"I think that's what they like about each other." Kit looked fondly at his lover. "Do you really not get the irony in your words?"

Romy gave Kit his perfected blank look.

"Babe," Kit said, chucking Romy under the chin with his knuckle. "You and I were as different as two people could be when we met."

Romy shook his head. "No. We're just alike."

"How can you say that?"

Romy took Kit's hand and put it over his heart without regard for who might be watching. "We might be different on the outside, but in here, we're the same."

"Another Hallmark moment," Kit said before his voice choked off. He took a shaky breath. "You're determined to give me diabetes, aren't you?"

"I have no ulterior motives. So about the concert...."

"We can't make it."

Romy's mouth dropped open. "What? Why not?"

"We'll be too busy."

"Doing what?"

"Soaking up sun in Cozumel."

"You're kidding me!"

"No, I'm not. It's all set. We drive to Galveston in the morning and leave for what the travel agent assures me is an unforgettable, all-gay cruise to Cozumel Island."

"I've always wanted to go there."

"I remember when you told me that."

Romy threw his arms around Kit. "It was luckiest day of my life when those ants clogged up your fuel filter."

"Hm, maybe this was their plan all along, the little matchmakers."

"They gave their lives for our happiness." Romy pretended to sob.

Kit kissed Romy. "Maybe we should erect a monument to those who gave all."

"Lunatic." Romy kissed Kit back. "We're too busy. We have to pack for Cozumel!"

CONNIE BAILEY is a Luddite who can't live without her computer. She's an acrophobic who loves to fly, a fault-finding pessimist who, nonetheless, is always surprised when something bad happens, and an antisocialite who loves her friends like family. She's held a number of jobs in many disparate arenas to put food on the table, but writing is the occupation that feeds her soul.

Connie lives with her ultralight designer husband at a small grass-strip airfield halfway between Disney World and Busch Gardens. Logic and reality have had little to do with her life, and she likes it that way.

Visit her blog at http://baileymoyes.livejournal.com/.

Also from CONNIE BAILEY

Until It's
Time To Go

Connie Bailey

http://www.dreamspinnerpress.com

Also from CONNIE BAILEY

TRUE BLUE

Connie Bailey

http://www.dreamspinnerpress.com

Connie Bailey

Something for Nothing

Also from CONNIE BAILEY

http://www.dreamspinnerpress.com

Also from CONNIE BAILEY

http://www.dreamspinnerpress.com

CONNIE BAILEY

*Kaji Sukoshi &
The Shining One*

http://www.dreamspinnerpress.com

Also from CONNIE BAILEY

http://www.dreamspinnerpress.com

Don't miss from CONNIE BAILEY

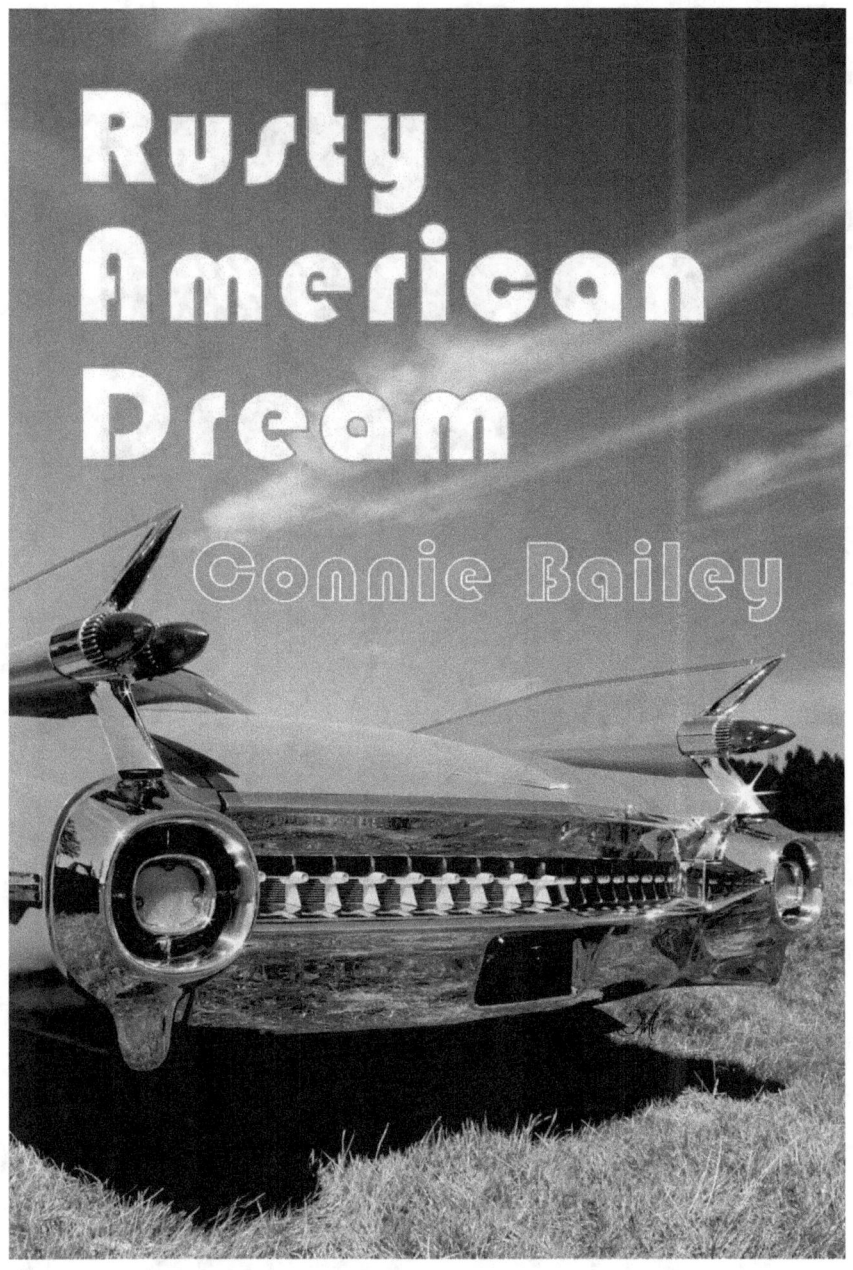

Rusty
American
Dream

Connie Bailey